Ge

Getting Schooled

When 26 year old Reese accepts a position as a grad assistant, she has no idea an unpleasant encounter with a student will lead to the discovery of what she calls "the trifecta": fine, intellectual, and a little bit rude – three qualities she finds irresistible in a man. She has no intention of doing anything with that discovery – nothing long term, at least. But everybody knows what happens to best laid plans.

Jason is a grown man. 28 years old, seasoned and scarred by his real-life experience in the world, he's at Blakewood

State University to finish his degree and move on. The last thing he's interested in is the female population on campus... but sexy, infuriating Reese might be a notable exception.

This isn't a story of opposites attract.

More like counterparts clash.

Neither of them is afraid to do battle, and neither is willing to back down. Love and war, win or lose... somebody's gonna end up getting schooled.

To every single person who has provided their time, energy, friendship, and love to me, through the course of writing this book.

To every reader who takes a chance on me with every new project.

To every person who didn't see fit to coddle me, or "play nice".

To every critic and naysayer.

Thank you.

Words can't express how appreciated you are.

one.

Reese

"This is part of why I want to reiterate and reinforce my previous point, that this author is, frankly, full of shit. He's using the fictional character of Vaughan to act out his absurdly patriarchal views of women as objects to be gawked at and abused for his sexual gratification, because in real life, the type of woman that Vaughan obtains would never give Cory Jefferson a second look. Welleducated, confident, worldly women don't tend to flock to selfimportant, borderline abusive assholes. At least, not in my experience.

Further, it's a glaring indication of self-hatred that none of the "beautiful" women in this piece are described as darker than a paper bag, have good old

"brown" eyes, or have hair any kinkier than a loose wave. Darker skinned women are consistently referred to as aggressive, ugly, low class, and uncultured. Vaughan has "relationships" with at least fifteen women through the course of this

"book", and ***none*** *of them have braids? Locs? A fro? A fade? In 2016? Come on. Cory Jefferson is as black as you can get without being blue, but he can't see the beauty in skin the color of anything except milk with a splash of coffee?*

That's not a preference – it's a pathology."

So… yeah.

This paper earns a goddamned bae-plus if you ask me.

I squeezed my thighs together, and let out a small, inaudible sigh as I focused on the essay filling the screen of my laptop. Propping my elbows on the desk in front of me, I folded my hands together, using them to support my chin as I lifted my eyes to the lecture hall full of varying shades of brown faces.

Which one of you is going to impregnate me with your socially-conscious babies?

Was it the caramel-toned cutie with the locs and the ankh tatted on his bicep?

Or Mr. Future Insurance Agent, who always came to class in polos and khakis?

Hmm.

Maybe the pretty boy with the mahogany skin and designer prescription frames?

Or, Mr. Black-in-Every-Way-Except-Race, with the exaggerated swagger that earned him a spot in the world of melanin-rich Greek life?

Yeah…

Probably the white boy.

I shook my head, and turned my attention back to the screen. They were students – I wasn't. At least not in the same sense as them. Nobody in this classroom, junior level course or not, was old enough for me to do anything except mumble about how "they didn't make them like that" back when *I* was a junior – a whopping five years ago.

There was a whole lot of fine in this lecture hall, sure. On the Blakewood State University campus, period. But looks aside, I preferred men with a little more seasoning.

A little more experience.

A little more *not* still living in the dorms or oncampus apartments.

A little more enlightened worldview.

Like whoever actually read more books than the ones on the required reading list, and retained enough to write this paper.

I let out another sigh.

It was really too bad.

I clicked in the margins of the document, opening a comment bubble.

"Excellent social commentary here,"

I started there and stopped, putting a completely unnecessary pen between my teeth, biting down as I carefully considered my words before continuing.

"Unfortunately, much of this doesn't fall within the bounds of the assignment. Scoring this based on the rubric you were provided, this paper wouldn't earn more than 68.75 out of a possible 100, if this were a final draft. Consider the following revisions for a higher score:"

I spent the next few minutes making suggestions in various places on the document, including a little reminder to focus on the work, not the author, even though his opinion was spot on, if you asked me.

At least I assumed the student was a "he".

Something in the linguistic choices and style screamed *male* to me, even though the name, J. Wright, did nothing to encourage that notion.

Whoever it was, they'd be busy this weekend making those revisions. They were smart to take advantage of the offer to send in a first draft for review, with the paper itself not being due until the following week. None of them were expected to actually be *good* writers yet – this was a junior level course. By the time they left, their skill level would hopefully be a different story, but for now, especially since it was still early in the semester, they got a few crutches.

I hit the "submit" button on my suggestions, waited to make sure they went through, and then closed the program as the class ended. I watched for a few seconds as the students packed up their laptops and began filing out, and then remembered I had things to do myself.

Pulling my bag onto the desktop, I closed my computer and shoved it inside, looking up as I felt the shift in energy of someone standing beside me.

"Reesie," my mother said, bending at the waist to shove her cell phone in front of me. "What is this? What is a *P-I-L-F*?"

I furrowed my eyebrows, reading the caption below the picture that filled most of the screen, of my mother at the BSU alumni cookout a few weeks before the semester started.

"Maaan, @profBryantBSU is fine af. #idontseearing #ageaintnothinbutanumber #throwindownaintnothinbutathang #PILF #BSUfinest"

My eyes went wide, and then darted up to the username who'd posted this – some kid, most likely from one of her freshman College Writing courses. The picture was pretty innocent, but my mother did look good. She was posing with two of her colleagues, smiling at the camera in an ikat-print romper that hit her mid-thigh. The halter style of the top completely covered her breasts, but her toned arms – and if she turned around, her back – were exposed. It was a tasteful outfit for the heat of summer, at an event where there had been ribs, beer, and an abundance of playing cards.

Imara Bryant *was* pretty damned fine, but I could admit to being biased. Copper-toned skin, thick lashes, a cute nose and full lips, all of which I'd inherited, made for an appealing package. Most mornings, she summoned me to the campus sidewalks to go running with her, and she was constantly on my ass about eating well and drinking enough water – her weapons in the battle against aging. Some of her almost-fifty years showed in the fine lines of her face, but as an overall package, mommy was winning.

Evidenced by this social media post.

I giggled a little as she peered over my shoulder, eyes narrowed in concentration behind her delicate glasses. "Mama, you know what a *milf* is, right?" She nodded.

“Well, looking at these context clues, I’d say a *pilf* is a “professor I’d like to fu—”

“I’m going to email this little boy’s mother!” she exclaimed in a loud whisper, glancing furtively at the students still exiting the class. “She had the nerve to contact me because I called him in during office hours to discuss why he can’t seem to focus in class. Well now I *see*!”

“Relax, mama.” I grinned, patting her on the arm as I stood and slung my laptop bag over my shoulder.

“Shouldn’t be this fly if you don’t want anybody to notice.”

I tossed her another smile before I pulled my cell out, my fingers flying over the screen as I texted my friend Devyn on the way out the door. Just as my thumb

went to the button to hit “send”, I collided with a warm body, and bounced back from the impact.

Looking up, I took in a tall body and broad shoulders, wrapped in the standard navy blue *Dickies* uniform of an auto mechanic. Reflexively, my eyes dropped to check for any grease or grime that may have gotten onto me, marring the summer white of the offshoulder peasant blouse I wore with jeans and flats. I’d been trying all day to keep it pristine, but it seemed like the entire campus was against me.

“Don’t worry,” a deep voice rumbled, edged with irritation. “I didn’t get anything on your… shirt.”

If there was ever an instant where it was possible for the word *shirt* to be an insult, this was definitely it. It rolled off his tongue like my carefully selected outfit was disgusting to him, like it didn’t even deserve to be considered as an article of clothing. I could admit that the gauzy cotton top was a little eclectic, but *damn.*

My eyes climbed higher, wanting to connect the frosty demeanor with a face, but he'd already brushed past me – not exactly rough, but certainly not gentle either – and the only things I caught were pecan-colored skin and a crisply lined fade.

"Excuse you!" I called at his retreating back, but he didn't bother to turn around, or otherwise acknowledge that I'd said anything. *Asshole.*

I stepped out of the doorway, out of the way of any other students who may have been on their way out. It was Friday, and the last class of the day, so the building was emptying quickly as everyone scurried toward their weekend plans. Raising my phone, I unlocked the screen and hit send on the message I'd been typing before rudeass bumped into me. I stuck my cell in the back pocket of my jeans, and was heading toward the glass doubledoors that led out of the building when Olivia turned the corner and almost walked right into me.

"Just the girl I wanted to see!" she said, her face lighting up as she pulled me into a hug. Olivia worked in

BSU's law library as a legal research librarian, though she looked nothing of the part. When I first met her, she was a solid slacks, solid blouse kind of girl. Over the years, she'd loosened up and developed a little more diverse sense of style. Improved fashion choices had brought out new confidence, new confidence brought out more ambition, and I mean… who *couldn't* use a little more ambition?

"What's up Liv?" I asked, stepping out of her embrace. "Hey, is my outfit ugly?"

She looped her arm through mine, joining me in exiting the library building, where the literature department was housed. "What? No, it's not. It's fly.

You're always fly. Why are you even asking me that?

Anyway. You're coming to *Refill* tonight, right?"

Refill was a popular hangout spot across town, too far from campus to attract the undergrad population. Sleek, modern décor, low key vibes, a liquor license, and a strictly enforced twenty-five or older policy made it ideal for the slightly bougie, professional late-twenties crowd.

My kind of crowd.

Still, I shook my head. "I honestly didn't plan to. Grayson finally got some time off, so he's supposed to be dropping by the house tonight."

Olivia abruptly stopped in her tracks, her pretty caramel toned face screwed into a little scowl. She had braids like mine, and swung them over her shoulder as she rolled her eyes. "Oh. You and Grayson are still a thing? Of course you're ditching your friends to hang with your man."

I sucked my teeth. "Uhh, back up. Have I not kicked it with you often over the last two months while he's been busy with this monster case? Don't try to play me like I'm the friend who disappears because she has a man, when you know that's not the situation."

There was silence between us for about two-

Mississippi because her frown softened. "I guess you're right, huh?"

"I don't have to guess," I chuckled, turning to continue my journey down the sidewalk. "I don't mean to duck out on you, but I haven't been able to spend any significant time with Grayson in months. Girlfriend duty calls."

Olivia let out a little sigh, then jogged a bit to catch up before falling into stride beside me. "I know, I get it. I was just hoping to have some company to go listen to Julian Black sing tonight."

I cringed. "*Oooh*, that was tonight?" Shit.

Julian Black was this generation's Joe, Tyrese, Usher, Ginuwine, you name it. Handsome, talented, the body of an Adonis, without the social media fuckery. So basically, full blown unattainable crush material that I was missing out on seeing live in favor of kicking it with

Grayson… and I wasn't sure I felt like it was worth it.

"Maybe you could bring Grayson with you? That way you get to see Julian, see Grayson, *and* not leave me hanging. Three birds, one stone."

I smiled. "As compelling as your argument is," I said, stopping at a crosswalk to let a car finish passing before I continued, "it's still a no. Grayson already says he wants to do something quiet, just me and him. I don't think he'd be too enthused if I tried to drag him out there.

Maybe next time."

Olivia groaned. "Okaaay, Have fun with your boo."

"I definitely plan to."

We split up and went our separate ways, and in my car, I stifled a yawn.

Truthfully, part of my reluctance to go to Refill tonight was rooted in the fact that I was straight up tired. Between the coursework to finish my MFA, and my responsibilities as a grad assistant, I was a busy girl. I cherished the time I had to chill and kick it with my friends, but I was glad for an opportunity to be laid up in manly arms, and have my booty rubbed until I fell asleep early.

I pulled up to the duplex I called home about twenty minutes later, and dragged myself and my bag out of the car. I plopped down on the couch to take off my shoes and then sat back, knowing that I wouldn't be able to stay there long.

This was one of few weekends that I didn't have any assignments due when classes resumed on Monday.

Still, it would be a good idea to get ahead, since I wasn't planning to go out anyway, and it would be a few hours before Grayson arrived.

My cell phone let out a melodic chime, and I reached for it, taking it out of my bag. I grinned when I saw the message from Devyn, the woman who owned the title of "best friend" in my life.

"Grayson is still a 'thing' around these parts? Ew. – Devyn."

Shaking my head, I thought about what I wanted to type back. Her ill feelings toward Grayson were firmly rooted in a conversation we'd had after his first month of scarcity. She'd gotten this weird look on her face when she asked me if I missed him and my answer was no, but it wasn't that big of a deal to me.

I'd never been the girl to be stuck under a man, vacuuming up his time. If he wanted to chill, fine. If not, I wasn't that pressed. Obviously, there were some boundaries and specific criteria to that, but in general, I wasn't too bothered about Grayson's absence. He was busy, I was busy. Shit happened when you were our age, finishing grad degrees, and starting careers.

Devyn wasn't convinced, but that was okay. Bestie or not, I didn't need her approval to continue a relationship with Gray. We talked, texted, grabbed lunch or dinner where we could, but between case filings, legal briefs, and traveling back and forth between here and Seattle to mollify some big shot client, his time was limited. Which was totally okay, cause I didn't have time for him to always be sniffing behind me either.

"Yes, Gray is still a thing, smart ass. I need SOMEBODY to stroke this kitty."

I preemptively chuckled, imagining her response, and then tapped on the blinking email notification at the top of my screen. Some of the messages were from classmates, exchanging notes, asking about assignments. I responded where necessary to those, and then moved to the ones from the program BSU used to allow professors to give feedback on student-submitted papers.

Because I was my mother's grad assistant, and had the responsibility of providing the critique for her Modern Black Literature course, any correspondence was first routed to me – not that the students knew that. I'd had to stop myself from bursting into laughter in the middle of her lecture more than once, reading some of the asinine excuses some people gave for late, or bombed assignments. And then I handed them their asses, because that's exactly what mama – ahem. *Professor Bryant* – would do.

One message in particular stood out, at least to my eyes.

"J. Wright" had responded to my feedback from earlier, and for some reason, I felt a little giddy as I clicked to open the message.

"I'd like to contest the assertion that my paper goes outside of the scope of the assignment. The ***book*** *goes outside of the scope of the assignment, because this isn't literature. It's presented as literary fiction, but it's a badly written hood novel with a heaping dose of magical realism,* ***at best.*** *It could be in the "black" section at the bookstore, with the title in blinged-out font and a halfnaked woman (with green eyes, long hair, and light skin) holding a gun. It would be a much better fit there."*

My eyes went wide, and I blinked a few times, reading the message again before a smile spread over my face, and I shook my head. Instead of replying from my phone, I pulled out my laptop and laid the phone down at my side. It took a few minutes to load my email up, but once I did, I quickly typed out a response.

"The assignment was not to analyze whether or not Mr.

Jefferson's work was suitable reading material for the class. It was to provide a critical analysis of said work. If you want to make the claim that ***City of Dreams*** *is not fit to be called literature, you can certainly do so. In your paper."*

I sat back, deciding to wait a few minutes to see if *J. Wright* was going to respond right away. Apparently, he wasn't drinking the Cory Jefferson Kool-Aid, and neither was I. He was being hailed – by "liberal" white people, grossly misogynist "enlightened" men, and the silly women who pandered to both – as some kind of literary messiah, but fuck that. I'd actually personally side-eyed my mother about this book choice, and gotten a laugh in response.

Every year, in the midst of the actually good books she required the class to read, she would throw in a choice that made my damned teeth itch. According to her, the goal was to help her students discern what was good literature and what wasn't. She'd assured me that *City of Dreams* was this year's "wasn't", and I was incredibly pleased to see that she'd taken my suggestion of doing a couple of her lectures on romance-centered novels.

But back to Corey Jefferson – I wasn't sure if his inclusion was having the desired effect, so far. It had been hard as hell for me to read some of those papers and not give the feedback that the student needed to jump off a cliff into a sea of dicks. Some of these kids actually agreed with Corey Jefferson's bullshit, and it made my head hurt.

My computer pinged, letting me know I had a new message, and my heart started beating a little faster when I saw *J. Wright* in the "from" box.

"Hey, my bad Professor B. I didn't mean to imply that you'd made a mistake in choosing the book. It's definitely an

eye-opener, even if I'd rather keep mine closed on this one. Still, message received.

In any case, I ***do*** *want to contest the assertion that my social commentary isn't suitable here.* ***City of Dreams*** *is a very, very widely read bestseller, with a huge marketing push of movies, merchandising, etc behind it.*

People are buying into these words like they're some type of law. This book, and the ideas and ideals it presents, absolutely have a social impact. I think exploring that as part of critiquing the overall work is valid."

I had to walk away from the laptop on that one. I considered calling "Professor B" to see what she thought, but I didn't want her peering at me over those glasses of hers, not saying anything, but questioning my competence anyway. On the other side of that, *she* would provide the final grade on the paper, with my notes and scoring provided as suggestions. Even if I said was accepting it, there was no guarantee she would agree.

But on the other side – yes, I was up to a thought triangle now – she rarely went against me. She actually tended to score things higher than me, so maybe I was worried for nothing.

I walked around my space, straightening up for Gray's arrival later, and then climbed into the shower.

Now that my apartment and I were clean, I felt better, and

I sat down in front of the laptop again, staring at my fingers as I considered my response. Finally, I typed something out.

"Cite your sources. Use direct quotes. Provide examples. Show context."

If J. Wright was so adamant, I'd give him the chance to make his case. Crush-worthy social and literary views or not… his ass had better write to impress if he wanted to earn a better grade.

two.

JASON

"Cite your sources. Use direct quotes. Provide examples. Show context."

I pushed out a heavy, relieved breath as I sat back in my chair, letting it swivel back and forth as I re-read the message on the screen. Those ten words had just saved me from having to cut a crazy amount of work from a paper that was due on Monday. Yeah, I had some work to do to address the other things the professor had pointed out, but those were no big deal. I could make those adjustment tonight when I got home, have my Saturday off to my damned self, and read over the paper again on Sunday.

"Hey, where are you? Jay?" *Shit.*

I closed out my email and slipped my phone back into my pocket as I hopped up from the chair. There was just enough time for me to look like I'd already been on my way out when my father, Joseph Wright Sr., rounded the corner.

"What are you doing back here in the break room?" he asked, wearing a little frown as he looked me over. "And why aren't you in the polo with the company logo?"

Because that shit looks wack, I thought, but didn't say. Instead, I just kind of shrugged as I slipped past him, and headed back to the glass-walled cubicle right up front that my father referred to as my "office", but felt more like a cage.

"Hold up," he called after me, and I stopped, pushing my hands into my pockets as I turned in his direction. "It's your lucky day… we had a mechanic call out, so—"

"Yes!"

I didn't even really need to hear the rest of what he said. I was already headed toward the back, toward the service center where I really wanted to be in the first place.

"*Slow down, son.*"

Again, I stopped. Turned to look my father in the eyes, because I already knew what was coming. "What, you don't even have two words to spare for your old man today?"

Oh.

Wait.

I wasn't expecting *that*.

Joseph Wright had never been a lovey-dovey guy, not with me or my brothers. He saved the mushy stuff for our mother – turned into a smooth-talking teddy bear when he interacted with her. For us boys though, it was always toughen up, less emotion, work harder, sweat more, better grades – normal shit, honestly. Looking back, I could see that he was careful not to talk down to us though, not to be too harsh, leading by example. He was raising men, not assholes, he said at least once a week, usually directed at me.

He swore up and down, backwards and forward that he'd been me, exactly, growing up. That my

"candor" as my mother referred to it, had come to me honest, passed down from him. That the sheer potency – his word choice – of my mother, once they met, had polished away the sharpest of the edges on his personality, made him a little easier, a little more smooth.

"I can't wait for you to meet your sandpaper, little boy," my mother, Priscilla, had dryly muttered to me one day, long past the time I was actually a little boy. I was home on leave, and she insisted I take one of her friend's daughter out.

I suffered through the date, with a girl whose jaw was stronger than mine and couldn't keep her clammyass hands to herself. I was nice-ish. I was polite to this girl. I drop her off, walk her to her door… and she snatches me by the collar, trying to get a kiss.

I got the whole fuck outta there, and I don't know what she told *her* mom, but her mom called *my* mom, and Priscilla Wright called me into her sewing room and just looked at me, with that quiet disappointment that stung a helluva lot more than anything my father ever said.

But, back to my point.

My father wasn't some talkative, sentimental guy. We often communicated in little more than a series of grunts that we each inexplicably understood.

When he stopped me, I was expecting to be admonished because I was wearing a mechanic's shirt, instead of the wack-ass white polo with the royal blue

J&P AUTO SALES logo embroidered on. He was always on me about presenting myself like a salesman, even at my blunt insistence that it wasn't what I wanted to do. But, it paid the bills and kept me out of my savings while I attended school, and he was generous enough to give me flexible hours.

What I hadn't expected was to look into my father's eyes and see genuine concern over my lack of communication today.

"Sorry Pops," I said, clapping him on the shoulder. "School on my mind. You good?"

"Are *you* good?" he countered back, not releasing me from his penetrating stare. "Ever since you've been back, you've been—"

"*Fine.* I'm fine, Pops. Okay?"

"You don't *seem* fine. I'm worried about you, son."

"Worried about who?"

I groaned at the sound of the voice behind us.

Here we fucking go…

"Why're you worried about Jay, Pops? What's going on? Jay, you good? You need me to look at—"

"*Nah,*" I insisted, turning to face my older brother, Joseph Jr. "I don't need you to look at anything,

Dr. Wright."

Joseph gave me a dry smile. "Ha ha. Funny. Are you sure—"

"*Yes*. Can I get out to the service center now?" I asked, addressing both men with the question. They exchanged a look, and Joseph Jr. gave Joseph Sr. a slight head nod that I guess they thought I couldn't see.

"Yeah, son. Go ahead," my father agreed, and I didn't waste any time taking advantage of the out, leaving them to discuss my demeanor. There was nothing to discuss though. I wasn't different, *they* were.

I'd only been home a few months, since right before the semester started, and had noticed it more and more in the time I'd been back. My family tiptoed around me in a way they hadn't before, always watching me, asking me how I was, like they expected any little thing to set me off into a panic attack or something.

I knew what they were worried about. PTSD, flashbacks, nightmares of kids with bombs strapped to their backs. All the shit American movie magic shoved down our throats as the reality of what deployment looked like, when the truth wasn't nearly as depressing or tragic, but somehow, simultaneously worse. I didn't know how to explain it, but the point was that none of that was happening with me. I was *good.*

I just needed my well-meaning family to realize that, and lay off, damn.

As soon as I stepped into the part of the dealership that housed the service center, I breathed in a deep sigh. The cloying smells of engine grease, brake dust, rubber, gasoline, and motor oil would send most people into a gagging, coughing fit, but it smelled like home back here to me.

The little BSU princess from earlier would probably die of shock.

A twinge of annoyance settled into my shoulders, remembering the way she'd recoiled at the sight of my mechanic's shirt. I wore it to class with some regularity, because it saved me time from going all the way home on the days I worked at the dealership. My clothes were clean though, because my mama raised me right. No, I wasn't on campus dressed to impress like the pretty boys she probably preferred, but that was the thing – I wasn't a boy. I was twenty-eight years old, just trying to take advantage of the military's generosity and get my damned degree so I could get the fuck out of there. I was surrounded by teenagers, and kids so barely into their twenties that they may as well be teenagers too.

But not the princess.

No, as annoyed as I'd been by that little accidental exchange in the classroom door, I couldn't deny that unexpected softness of her body against mine had felt good. It wasn't the first time I'd seen her – she was always in the lecture hall on Fridays, sitting at the table next to Professor Bryant, looking good as hell.

Pretty copper-brown skin, big brown eyes, and a sexy ass mouth. She had her hair done in thick, jet-black braids that hung past her waist, grazing the soft curves of her hips. The obvious hint that she was older than the girls of campus lied in the fact that she was a grad assistant. She had to have at least graduated with a bachelor's to be in the position she was, which meant at least twenty-one, twenty-two, but I suspected even older than that. Something in her vibe – easy, breezy, bougie as hell – spoke to a level of confidence the younger women didn't seem to have.

Not to mention, I'd heard the little smartass remark she hurled at my back after we bumped into each other. Even though I hadn't responded, only a selfassured woman fired back like that, despite the fact that she was clearly the one at fault.

Aiight.

So… maybe that's not completely accurate.

Maybe she was too busy looking at her phone to watch where she was going.

Maybe *I* was too busy looking at her ass, too distracted by the sliver of brown skin between the top of her jeans and the hem of her shirt – she had those little dimples, the thumb placement guides, you know? – to watch where *I* was going.

So maybe it was both of our fault.

But the princess didn't have to act like I was covered in grease and grime either, so there was that. She

wasn't into men who got their hands dirty, and I wasn't into stuck up women.

The end.

I finished up my shift at the service center, and went home, dodging my father and brother on the way out. There, I pulled out some leftover chicken and rice, and stuck it in the oven to heat while I got in the shower.

Afterwards, I set up my laptop at my desk, and sat in front of the computer with my dinner while I worked on my paper.

While I *aced* my paper.

What the fuck is this?!

I sat back from my computer screen in disbelief, staring at the score at the bottom of my paper for Modern Black Lit. I blinked, looked at it again, and then looked around me, searching for someone to confirm whether or not I was seeing what I thought I was seeing.

82.5%

Yeah, yeah, that was a passing score. A lot of people would have been fine with that, but I wasn't, because for one – I wrote the shit out of that paper. Two – a "B" was aiight in passing, but the final grade for the course was based on a cumulative score, not weighed by the letter grade. It was too early in the semester to be dragging my score down. And three… *I wrote the shit out of that paper.*

Wearing a scowl, I scrolled furiously through the paper, reading the comments. I was in the library, studying fucking thermodynamics for a test later in the week. But nah, I heard the little ping from the email, and had to check it. Now, I was pissed off and worried about my GPA over a class that didn't have shit to do with the degree I was seeking.

I wanted to get a little bit pissed at my advisor, but it wasn't his fault I was one of the last students to register. I was lucky to get into *any* classes, let alone the ones I actually needed, that weren't just filling out my electives. I was known to pick up a book or two in my spare time, so the last-minute opening in Modern Black Lit worked for me. Added bonus: Professor Bryant was grown-woman fine, which made it easy as hell to pay attention in class. Things were good.

Until now.

My eyes narrowed as I read over the comments. *Underdeveloped thesis, rambling paragraphs, how does this connect to your (underdeveloped) thesis? Citation needed, blah, blah.* Ultimately, she left a nice little note at the end about how this was a strong effort, but "Strong

Effort" and "82.5%" didn't compute. At least not to me.

Since I was already in the building, I packed up my stuff, printed a copy of the paper, and went upstairs to

Professor Bryant's office. I didn't know her schedule, if she had office hours or was in class, but if I could catch her, I wanted to talk in person about the paper.

The door was already open when I got there, so I stuck my head in and looked around. Professor Bryant's office was large, enough to comfortably fit two desks and still look spacious. The larger desk, undoubtedly hers, was unoccupied.

The princess sat behind the other one.

She had her head down, scribbling away in a notebook. Skinny purple headphone cords disappeared behind her braids, and I had to stop myself from staring too hard at her round, plump titties, filling out the front of a royal blue Blakewood tee shirt, with a v-neck.

I cleared my throat, and her head popped up, eyes wide as she slammed her notebook shut and yanked her earbuds out. "Can I help you?" she asked, sounding a little flustered as she stood up.

It hadn't been quite a week yet since we bumped into each other, and I hadn't seen her since then. Today was Thursday – she would be in the lecture hall tomorrow, but somehow this was a little different. Just me and her, relative privacy… why the hell did she have to be this fine?

"Uhh," I started, shaking my head a little to clear away filthy thoughts about my hands and her hips. "I was looking for Professor Bryant."

"She's not here."

I raised an eyebrow. "Yeah, I can see that. Can you tell me when she'll be back?"

"Her office hours are posted there on the door for convenience."

"That's not what I asked you."

The princess crossed her arms over her chest, which didn't do anything except push her titties together, making it harder not to stare. "You're the guy that bumped into me the other day, aren't you?"

I smirked. "Nah. You bumped into *me*, but I can see how you might think otherwise."

She rolled her eyes, muttering something that sounded suspiciously like *"this motherfucker"* under her breath before she turned her gaze back toward me, her expression completely disinterested. "What do you want?"

"To talk to the professor."

"About?"

"My grade on this paper."

A nasty little grin spread across her face. "What's wrong? Did you fail?"

"*No.*" I scoffed, shook my head. "I didn't fail, I'm just not happy with the grade. When will Professor Bryant be available to talk about it?"

"She won't. Scores are final."

Narrowing my eyes, I stepped forward into the office. "I want to hear that for myself. When will she be available today?"

"It's a waste of both of your time. She's not changing the grade."

I swallowed hard, feeling the patience ooze out of me more with every second that passed. "When can *I* talk to *her*?"

"Professor Bryant doesn't have office hours on Thursdays."

Any possible hint of amusement drained off of my face, and went onto hers. The princess's expression was high-fructose corn syrup sweet, and her eyes were sparkling with barely constrained laughter.

I blew out a deep breath, with a dry chuckle as I shook my head. "You couldn't have said that shit at first, huh?"

She shrugged, and then stepped around the desk, strutting in my direction. I watched her ass as she passed, then brought my eyes back up as I turned around. She stopped at the door, pointing to a laminated sheet taped to it. "Like I said – her schedule is posted on the door. Can you see it here?

With OFFICE HOURS right here across the top, in these big ass letters?"

"Man, whatever," I said, tossing my printed copy of the paper onto Professor Bryant's desk. I strolled out, stopping right in front of the princess. I breathed in, and whatever perfume she was wearing, some mixture of jasmine and sandalwood and vanilla, made me damn near forget what I was about to say. "Just tell her Jason stopped by, if you're seeing her today, aiight?"

She had her back pressed to the door, staring up with this bored expression. "Aiight, *Jason.*" She sidled out of her position between me and door, gripping the knob in her hand as I stepped back, into the hall. "But just so you know… grades are final."

I didn't even have a chance to respond before she closed the door in my face.

three.

I closed the door, and locked it too, for good measure. I needed that strong separation between me and "Jason". I was hoping more than anything to shut off his presence, his smell, the inexplicable heat between my legs that had grown hotter and hotter as we went back and forth.

It didn't work.

I hung my head, pressing my back to the door. It was so very, *very* like me to be turned on by a rude ass. It wasn't just a one-time thing anymore, so calling him an asshole last week felt pretty damned accurate now. I put my thumbs to my nipples, trying to calm them down, and hoping that my strategically crossed arms had hidden them from Mr. Stick-Up-His-Butt's view.

The last thing I needed was one of my mother's students thinking he had some kind of effect on me. Just because his skin was mouthwatering like roasted pecans, and his chiseled features gave me GQ vibes, and that neatly-groomed-but-scruffy thing he had going in the facial hair area was swoon-worthy, and his biceps were down right lickable, and—*shit.*

Ugggggh!

Why did he have to be so insolent and fine? Two qualities that I generally avoided in men, because they were shamefully irresistible. But, *haha,* lucky me. Good old Jason was undoubtedly the author of one of the papers I suffered through, since he was up here complaining about his grade.

That was a turn off to end them all.

With a smirk on my face, I marched over to my mother's desk and snatched up the printed copy of his paper, flipping to the end to read the grade.

82.5.

Wait… what?

I read those numbers again, to make sure I was seeing them right, and there it was again – nowhere near a failing grade. I skimmed over the comment my mother had left at the end, then moved my eyes to the top of the page to read a little of the content.

Holy shit.

The pages fluttered out of my hands. I didn't need them to know what words would come next, because I'd read *that* paper so many times, for my own enjoyment, that I practically knew the words from memory.

The first page had landed face up on the desk, right in front of me. The program that I used to critique papers removed the title block, to help preserve student anonymity. All I ever (usually) knew was the student's last name and first initial, and at a black college, come on. We had so many Johnsons and Browns and

Washingtons and Jacksons that knowing someone's surname and first initial really didn't mean you knew shit. But I *did* know something.

I knew now that the J. Wright I was scholastically crushing on was the same dude who'd had the nerve to be pissy with me after we bumped into *each other*. The same one who'd gotten an attitude when I answered his question, on my damn day off. I wasn't even supposed to be here today – I was doing mama a personal favor since she was without her car.

"It'll only take ten minutes Reesie, promise." Yeah.

And those ten minutes had cost me the blissful ignorance that the refined, progressive, possibly loc'd,

Nubian intellectual I'd imagined was actually some discourteous mofo named *Jason.*

And... I wasn't turned off by it. No, no, the exact opposite.

Another, less insane girl might have considered this a waste of appeal. Handsome and smart were universally appealing, but being a jerk was usually a deal breaker.

Not your silly ass though, Reese.

Nope.

That little hint of savagery was like catnip to me. Our little exchange, paired with his gorgeous face, already had me hot and bothered, but *now*? Knowing that he read actual books – more than just for class. He *had* to, to have a worldview like that – and understood them well enough to make cogent literary and social criticisms about those books?

It brought the teensy, tiniest little tear to my eye.

Because *this* man was the friggin' holy trifecta. I mean, holy trinity. I mean… *shit.*

He had my head all messed up.

- & -

"Reesie, were you rude to one of my students?"

My eyes went wide, and stayed glued to the road in front of me as I pulled to a stop at a red light.

Goddamnit he snitched on me… excellent move.

"Mommy whhhaaa? Who would tell you such a thing?"

She sucked her teeth. "So you were then."

I cringed a little, turning my head to stare out the driver side window as I waited for the light to change.

My mother didn't say anything else, but that silence weighed on me more than words, and she knew it. I peeked up at the light – *still red, damn!* – and then over at her, to see her phone in her hands.

Guess *Jason* had put those writing skills into an email, which I would pay good money to read. He didn't even know Corey Jefferson and he'd gutted that man's entire literary existence. Was it bad that I got a little bit aroused thinking about how he'd probably filleted me in the email to my mother?

"It really wasn't anything that big, I promise."

I glanced up at her, noting the censure in her eyes before I turned back to the road, just in time for the light to turn.

"That's interesting, because based on this email…"

"What does it say?" I asked, trying not to sound too giddy.

"Well, Mr. Wright is rather wordy – part of the problem with his paper – so how about I just give you the highlights? "*Earlier this afternoon, I had a startlingly negative interaction with the young woman working as your grad assistant. She was flippant, confrontational, and offensive, all in response to a humble, respectful request.*""

I rolled my eyes. *Startlingly negative? Flippant? Offensive? Humble, respectful request?* He was laying it on as thick as unstirred natural peanut butter.

"*When asking when I could get in contact with you, her response was unhelpful, and as we continued interfacing, progressed to openly vicious. She insulted my intellect when I mentioned wanting to speak with you about my grade, and I can't remember the exact words, but I believe it was something along the lines of, "Why, dumbass? What are you even doing here? Your stupid ass failed, didn't you?*""

"Okay *wait* a minute," I giggled, barely keeping myself from breaking into a howl of laughter. "I did *not* say that to him, oh my God!"

"I don't know Reesie, sounds like you…" "*Mommy!*"

"Hmm?"

"You really believe I said that to some random student?!"

"Well…"

"I would *never—*"

"Oh calm down little girl," my mother laughed, and I glanced over at her again as I made a right turn. "I know you didn't say those *exact* words… but I also know *you*. Mr. Wright is exaggerating, I'm sure, but I want you tell me why you're arguing with the students."

"*He started it*," I mumbled under my breath, instantly feeling sixteen instead of twenty-six. "I was in there getting those email addresses and stuff for you when he came in, saying he was looking for you. I told him your office hours were printed on the door, and he got smart with me!"

"And what did you do?"

Her voice was stern, and internally, I groaned. "I got smart back. But you have to understand, he bumped into me last week, and totally acted like it was my fault!"

"So that's a good reason for you to forget that you *work* for the university, and should remain professional when you're interacting there?"

I sighed. "No. It's not."

"Mmhmm. Maybe you should have thought about that, because getting reported to your boss, or your boss's boss, isn't going to look good when you need references. It's a hurdle to climb. You're a grown woman, I shouldn't have to clean up your messes anymore. And trying to explain to my department chair why you shouldn't get a formal reprimand, or worse, be fired, is exactly that – a mess."

"No," I said immediately, shaking my head even though my eyes were on the road. "You don't have to do that mama. You did enough by convincing them that I was a worthy hire, that it wasn't nepotism with me being your daughter. I don't want them looking at you any kind of way. I didn't have to go there with him, so if a formal reprimand is what would happen to anybody else, that's just the punishment I'll have to take."

I was right on the edge of tears, but swallowed them, even though they were sharp and bitter in my throat. Emailing my mother – though I doubt he knew *that* part, just that she was my boss – with that exaggerated account of what happened was one thing. Reporting me to the department was a whole other, fucked up thing. Still… I could have kept my mouth shut.

"I appreciate the maturity in that, Reesie. The only reprimand you're getting this time is a verbal one, from me. *Play nice with the students*, no matter how much they work your nerves. You want to be in front of a classroom full of adults someday, you're going to have to learn. Mr. Wright could have easily forwarded this to Dr.

Bradley too. Lucky for you, he didn't."

Relief swept through me as I pulled to the last traffic light before I would turn into the parking lot of our destination. I leaned forward, briefly touching my head to the steering wheel before I sat back with a sigh. "Point taken."

"Mmmhmm. I'm honestly surprised at you. I mean, I know you have that spitfire streak in you from your father, but at work? With a student?"

I blew out another sigh, shaking my head. "I surprised myself. He just… brought something out of me."

My mother chuckled. “Uh huh. I just bet he did.” “And what does *that* mean?!” I gasped.

“Little girl I’ve seen Jason Wright, and I’m not blind! And I’ve seen you fawn over his writing. A *90* on that paper? Seriously?”

I shrugged. “I thought it was good.”

“It wasn’t 90 points worth of good. You can’t let your little punany grade papers Reesie.”

I burst out laughing. “Seriously, mommy?”

“As a heart attack.”

I was still grinning as I pulled into a parking space and turned off my car. “I didn’t even know who he was to connect the face to the paper.”

“Whatever you say. And you *fought* with him too? That’s another thing you get from your father. Always want to fight with somebody, because afterward...” She trailed off, with a dreamy look on her face and made a noise in her throat. “I definitely miss that *afterward* part.”

“*Ewwww,*” I said, even though I grinned. “Don’t nobody want to think about you and my daddy, and don’t nobody want to think about some young behind college boy.”

My mother smirked. “Jason Wright is a nontraditional student, my dear. He’s *twenty-eight*.”

I almost made the same sound in my throat that she’d made a few moments earlier. *No wonder* he was so fine. He was a grown man, with that fuzzy-sexy five o’clock shadow, and hands that were big, and probably a little rough, and he was so... *sturdy* when we bumped into each other, that he hadn’t even moved. And despite my visceral, reflexive reaction to his mechanic's shirt, he smelled clean enough to wrap myself in and snuggle up.

And... a man who knew how to make a car purr could probably make a kitty purr too.

Don't you have a boyfriend? "Huh?"

"I said are you ready to go in?" My mother called from the other side of the car. She was already out, standing beside the car and peeking in at me.

"Oh! Yeah!"

I quickly got myself out of the car, taking a deep breath as I hit the button on my key fob to lock the doors.

"So... how did you reply to his message?"

"Who?"

"*Jason.*"

"Oh!" My mother grinned as she pulled her phone from her purse, and then hit a few buttons before she began to read. "*Mr. Wright, I am deeply regretful that you had that experience. I'll be speaking with Reese about it, and will make sure that you receive an apology from her for her actions—*"

"Say what now?"

"Uh huh. Now hush, and let me finish. *I'm surprised that Ms. Alston would act in such a manner, especially when she was an advocate for your paper to receive a higher grade. Unfortunately, I do not agree with her assessment. Simply work harder, Mr. Wright. The potential is there. If you have further questions or concerns, I'll be available after class tomorrow. Have a good weekend.*"

I shook my head. "I tried to tell him that."

"I know. He said that your words were *something like, "Ain't no grade change, bih!",* whatever the heck that means."

My eyes damn near bugged out of their sockets, and I stopped in my tracks as we headed for the front door. "He actually wrote that?!"

"Yes. And judging by your reaction, I'm starting to think he wrote the email knowing you would see it," she said, eyebrow raised.

I squared my shoulders and shook my head, trying not to smile. I would bet money that Jason Wright knew exactly what he was doing, and it was working, because my little twisted crush wasn't dying down.

I finally looked my mother in the eyes as we walked through the door of J&P Auto Sales, ignoring their amused light. "Maybe so, mama. Maybe so."

- & -

"Do you even know that man's last name mama?"

I teased, grinning at my mother's obvious excitement as she relaxed into the passenger seat of my car.

"I'm sure I'll find out when he calls," she quipped back, and laughed.

"Alright then. I guess you've still got it."

We'd just stepped out of J&P Auto Sales, and from the beginning, she'd been a goner – for the purchase of a car, and for the dealership's silver fox owner.

The moment we stepped through the door and he spotted her, I'd watched his eyes light up as he damn near sprinted to get to her first, before the other salesmen. He was a nice looking guy, and exactly my mother's type. Tall, smooth dark skin, and well groomed facial hair. The salt and pepper look was gravy.

"How are you ladies doing today?" he asked, in a deep voice with a little hint of rasp, and I could swear my mother shivered. He'd addressed us both, but was looking only at her as he extended his hand. "I'm the *J* in J&P

Auto, Joseph senior."

"Hello Joseph." She'd regained her composure, and straightened her shoulders, putting on a look best described as sensually aloof. She ran a free hand through her short-cropped curls – Joseph was still holding the other one – and pinned him with those big brown eyes. "What does the *P* stand for?"

Joseph's face dropped a little bit, in a hint of sincere sadness. "Priscilla. My late wife."

I'm pretty sure the word *"wife"* registered in my mother's brain first, because for about half of a second, her face was pulled into a scowl. Then the rest of the words hit, and her expression softened into sympathy.

Sensual sympathy, if that was a thing.

She stepped a little closer to him, covering their – *still* – clasped hands with her other one. "I'm sorry. I didn't mean to bring up a sensitive topic."

"Oh, it's no trouble at all." The smile came back to his face, warmer than ever. "She lived a wonderful, full life. Was a partner in this business, gave me three sons, thirty-six years of marriage. The last four years have been hard, but she's in a better place than here now, having a grand old time. Looking down on us, expecting us to do the same."

Wait... was that a hint that...?

"And what was your name?" He asked, smoothly flitting to the next thing.

"Imara Bryant."

"*Beautiful* name. Very fitting."

Oh my God. If her skin was lighter, she'd be friggin' beet red.

"What can I do for you today, *Imara*?"

My mother's name rolled off his tongue like he was making love to it, and my eyes went wide. *Like, right here in the dealership, bruh?* I thought, but knew ten times better than to say out loud. Besides, my mother was eating it up, and I had to admit that Mr. Chocolate was smooth. She had a big grin stuck on her face, and it took me a moment to realize she hadn't answered. I shook my head.

"A car," I said, speaking up for the first time, and mama *and* black George Clooney looked at me like they'd forgotten I was there. "She's here for a car. Remember, mama?"

"Ah." She gave Joseph a sweet – *sensual* sweet – smile. "Yes. I need to buy a car." So she bought a car.

And she *actually* got a good deal, according to my frantic blue-book valuing from my cell phone while Joseph sweet-talked her into a sleek black luxury vehicle(which she already wanted before we came to the dealership), and out of her phone number. The car stayed at the dealership to get some adjustments to the trim package, so I was driving her back home, and teasing her the whole way.

Even though it was a happy moment, I shuddered thinking about the reason she needed the new car in the first place. A few weeks ago, she'd been heading to go pick up her best girlfriend for a spa weekend. Some idiot got impatient and ran a red light as she was making a turn, and ended up t-boning her, on the passenger side.

Luckily, she'd walked away from the accident, with nothing more than a few bumps and bruises. But a car accident had taken my father seven years ago, and I couldn't help thinking about what might have happened if the car had been going faster, or hit on the driver's side, or…

I blinked back tears.

That *hadn't* happened.

I'd lost my father, but my mother was still here, and I cherished the hell out of that. She could be tough on me sometimes, but she was also my biggest supporter – evidenced by the position I had as her grad assistant anyway. She swore she'd chosen me based on merit, and had welcomed the challenge of getting me approved by the department. It wasn't that I thought I'd gotten some benefit by being her daughter, it was the exact opposite.

With the type of shit she knew about me, I would have expected her to gleefully choose someone else. But she didn't hold it against me. She chose me despite my history, because I was well-qualified. Or maybe because despite my history, I'd gotten qualified.

All of which could have easily not mattered if my little "conversation" with Jason Wright had gone anywhere beyond an email to the professor.

Yeah, it had been exciting to spar with him, but my mother was right – I *worked* at the college. That was no place for me to make business matters personal, or pick at him for my own entertainment. So, from now on, any interactions that related to my work as a grad assistant, *especially* on campus, would be strictly professional.

Even with "J. Wright."

Starting with that stupid ass apology.

four.

JASON

"Mr. Wright, may I have a moment of your time?"

Here we go…

I stopped in my tracks, turning to face the woman I now knew to be Reese. She had those big brown eyes of hers pulled wide, in an innocent expression that caught me off guard. I'd honestly been shocked last night when Professor Bryant emailed me back. Even *more* surprised to find out that: she was making Reese apologize, and that the princess had wanted to give me a higher score on the paper. That last little tidbit made me think that my strategy of emailing the professor hadn't been the right approach.

Or maybe it had, because I was about ninety percent sure we were about to go at it again. There was no way she was taking this "apology" shit lying down.

She tipped her head, urging me to quiet corner of the lecture hall as most of the students began to file out. I followed her, curious about what was happening next, and because, well… ass. Plenty of it, clad in jeans that fit her like a second skin. When she turned to face me, I followed the tiny straps of her shirt down to where her neckline dipped in the middle, showing just a hint of what had to be, wrapped in luscious skin like hers, beautiful breasts.

They hadn't looked *this* good in that tee shirt yesterday.

"Hey…," she said, and I brought my eyes up to her face. "About yesterday, in Professor Bryant's office?

Uh… she talked to me, about the email you sent. I know I can be a little abrasive sometimes, and some people are just much more sensitive to that than others. So, I shouldn't be speaking that way to anyone, not while I'm in official capacity here. I was completely out of line, and I want to apologize for hurting your feelings like that."

I tipped my head to the side. "Wait, hurting my feelings?"

"And I'm sorry," she continued, like I hadn't said anything, with the same placid expression on her face. "For any damage I may have done to your self-esteem. Students of *all* levels of intellect and ability are welcome here at BSU, and we can certainly make any accommodations your therapist or physicians may feel like you need. I'm sorry I gave you the impression otherwise."

"Wait, *what*? Let's back up. You didn't *hurt my feelings*, first of all."

Our little exchange in the office hadn't been serious enough for me to try to get her in trouble *or* for my damned feelings to be hurt about it. What *had* happened was a realization that to her, we were playing a game, starting from when we bumped into each other. Her next move was the flexing she'd done in Professor Bryant's office. Mine was emailing the professor.

In my mind, the professor would look at it, tell Reese to stop being an asshole, and then the next move would be on her. I'd thought about it long and hard, and it was, to me, the obvious path. I wasn't about to purposely bump into her again, and there was honestly nothing to insult. Our only connection was this classroom, and I was trying to see what the princess was made of.

"Oh, Mr. Wright," she sighed, with a sympathetic tilt of her head. "It's nothing to be embarrassed about. I was *so mean* to you, and that's not okay. I'm ashamed of myself for bullying you like that."

After those words dropped from her lips, her mouth spread into another syrupy smile, and I knew right then exactly what was happening. "I just want you to know," she continued, in the same sweet voice, "That I will never, *ever* engage you in that way on this campus again." She pushed a handful of her braids over her shoulder, then put her hand lightly on my bare arm. "You have a great weekend, Mr. Wright."

The classroom was empty now, and Reese didn't even look back as she grabbed her bag from her desk and sashayed out. *Have a great weekend* was what actually came out of her mouth, but the words may as well have been: *Your move, motherfucker.*

As far as I was concerned?

Game on.

- & -

Kicking it with my brothers and father wasn't exactly my idea of an exciting Friday night. But, with most of the people I considered friends either still in the military or scattered in other parts of the country, and no girlfriend, it wasn't like I just had a list of other things to do popping off.

So, it was just us guys.

The dealership was closed for the night, Joseph Jr. had the night off from the hospital, and even Mr. Bestseller, aka my middle brother, Justin had made time from writing to come and kick it. We were spread around the living room, with a coffee table full of pizza and wings, and preseason NFL football on my father's big flat screen, in the house we'd grown up in.

"Man, I hope Jordan Johnson keeps up this type of energy all season," Justin said around a full mouth, catching an olive from his pizza slice before it could hit the floor. "Connecticut loves getting their wide receivers from BSU, huh?"

Both brothers looked at me, but I shrugged. "Man, I guess. What do I look like, the BSU expert or something?"

"Well Blakewood *is* going to be your alma mater isn't it, college boy?" Joseph mushed the side of my head as he passed me heading into the kitchen, and I couldn't help it – I smiled. I may have complained about it being a "boring" Friday night, but I mean... these were my brothers.

I sat through a few more minutes of playful ribbing before I acknowledged that BSU *did* consistently put out some of the best wide receivers in the league. Jordan Johnson, Tariq Evans, and there was a kid whose name I couldn't remember getting ready to win a Heisman – also a product of Blakewood State University. A couple of moments after that, my father came jogging down the stairs, and I let out a low whistle.

"Daaamn. What's the occasion Pops?" I asked, putting a bottle of beer to my lips.

"Yeah," Justin added. "I thought we were watching a football game, not posing for GQ."

Joseph Sr. had come downstairs in dark slacks, dress shoes, and a deep blue, form-fitting tee shirt that showed off his successful avoidance of a beer belly. He had a blazer in his hands, and shook his head as he started to put it on.

"The occasion," he said, adjusting his lapels, and tugging his sleeves down, "Is that your old man has a date."

For about five seconds, a thick silence filled the room. I looked back and forth between my brothers, and they looked exactly like I felt – stunned.

My mother's death had hurt all of us, deeply, but nobody felt it like my father did. "Cilla", as he called her, was the love of his life, and for the first year after she passed, he was a complete wreck. I took the longest amount of leave I could to come home, and together, my brothers and I had taken care of him, because he wouldn't do it for himself. The business, his health, nothing. We'd had to step in to basically keep him alive.

The second year was a little better. He was functioning, but it was obvious he missed her. The third year brought a major improvement, and this year, he actually seemed to be coming alive again. But this was the first we'd heard of a *date.*

All three of us hopped up, and all started talking at once.

"Who is she?"

"When did this happen?"

"Are you sure you're ready?"

"Where are you going?"

"When are you coming home?"

"I thought you were kicking it with us tonight?"

My father shook his head, grabbing his keys from the hanger beside the door as he smiled. "Y'all grown asses don't need a chaperone to watch TV, I'm coming home when I get ready to come home, and I met her at the dealership yesterday. I'm taking her to the little jazz spot downtown, and… no, I'm not sure I'm ready. But only one way to find out."

We were silent for another few moments as we absorbed the answers to his questions, and then I nodded.

"Aiight. I think I like it. It's time you got back out there."

"Agreed," Joseph said. "What's her name? Did you look her up?"

Dad scowled. "*Look her up*? I'm old school, son. We didn't need any TweetBook, and Facegram, and

Insta-google, and all that crap. You see a pretty girl, you ask her out, you show her a good time. Call her on the phone. Woo her. That's all. What am I looking her up for?"

"Uh, to find out about her?" Justin's expression was confused as he eyed my dad, and my dad's expression was confused as he eyed Justin.

"Or," he said, "I could – and this is just the crazy notion of an old man – talk to her. Ask questions. Get to know the woman in her own words."

Joseph scoffed. "People lie all the time. What if this woman is a gold-digger or something?"

"That would be great. I need somebody to help me dig, maybe we'll find some."

I chuckled at Joseph and Justin's baffled expressions, then turned to my father, clapping him on the shoulder. "Hey… is she fine?"

His eyes lit up, and a goofy sort of grin spread across his lips. "Oh yes. Fine as bumblebee fuzz. Fine as a well-aged Bordeaux." He glanced down at his wrist. "And I do *not* want to keep a woman like that waiting, so… I'll see you boys later."

"Wait a minute," Joseph said, holding up a hand. "You haven't told us her name."

"Because it's not your business." Joseph Sr. smiled, and then gave us a little salute. "Don't wait up." My brothers kinda stood there for a few seconds after the door closed behind him, both looking shellshocked. I just shook my head, making my way back into the living room, grabbing a fresh beer, and piling my plate with wings before they got too cold.

Justin and Joseph joined me a moments later, still looking dazed.

"Y'all chill," I said, chuckling as I turned my attention back to the game. "I'm sure she's just some sweet church lady that came by for a car. He's growner than all of us. He'll be fine."

Justin let out a heavy sigh, then sat back. "So y'all don't think it's kind of… fast?" He was the one who'd asked my dad if he was really ready to be out there again like that.

Joseph saved me the trouble of answering. "It's been four years. Nah, I don't think it's fast. He's probably lonely."

"I don't mean fast like *that*," Justin scoffed. "I'm saying… just last year he couldn't even talk about her without tearing up, and now he's all excited about going on a date?"

I shrugged. "That's probably why. I mean, we all know he loved the hell out of mama, but there's always a point where you have to kinda let go of the past. Figure out how to live with what you've got now. I mean, come on… *I* know that shit better than anybody. Let Pops live.

We all remember what it was like when he wasn't trying to, right?"

That question was met with somber nods from Joseph and Justin, and they exchanged a glance with each other before they looked back to me.

"Aiight *baby* brother," Joseph grinned. "I guess you might have something rolling around in that big ass head after all."

And just like that, we were off my dad's business, and back on each other. Our attention drifted back to the game as the night wore on, and *my* attention wandered as the Connecticut Kings pulled off another win. A sports reporter stopped Jordan Johnson to talk, and she asked what he thought about BSU's prospects for the college season. I only vaguely cared about that, but the mention of BSU put something else on my mind.

I wondered what Friday night was looking like for a certain BSU princess.

"Bitch I will *kill you.*"

Those words were immediately followed by a sharp swat to my hand.

I snatched it back with an exaggerated "*Owww!*" and then slumped against my arm of the couch, scowling at my best friend. "It was an honest mistake!"

"The hell it was," she said. "Ten in the box, and your greedy ass already had six. This one is *mine.*" She took a vicious bite, her chew slow and exaggerated, with plenty of sound effects as she savored the last wing. I crossed my arms, pouting as I turned back to the preseason football game on the screen.

"Supposed to be my friend, treating me like a goddamned animal in my own house. Hmph!"

Devyn sucked her teeth, then took another bite of the wing. "I hear you over there, crazy."

"That's the whole point," I laughed. "Hey… would it be like… *too* greedy of me to order another box of wings?"

She lifted an eyebrow. "Only if it would be too greedy of *me* to help you eat them."

"Okay so then not at all."

I reached for my phone and placed the order right as the game ended, and fine ass Jordan Johnson ended up on my screen. We'd actually started BSU together in the same freshman class, and shared a few courses. I left shortly after that, and by the time I came back, he was already the resident college football hero of the school.

"Hey, you work tomorrow, don't you?" I asked, even though I already knew the answer. Devyn was a nurse, and she was almost always at work on Saturdays, a twelve hour shift that started at two in the afternoon.

"Of course." She sighed, then relaxed back into the couch cushions with her feet up on the ottoman and the silky, honey-blonde strands of her chin-length bob covering her face. "But I did I tell you I applied to University hospital?"

I sat straight up, and screamed. "You did?! Yesss!"

Devyn peeked at me through her hair, and shook her head. "I knew you weren't going to leave me alone unless I did it, so… yeah. We'll see what happens."

"You'll get the job is what's going to happen," I gushed. I'd been on Devyn about applying at the newer, state-of-the-art hospital for years now, but she was comfortable at the small hospital a county over. She made decent money, and had good relationships with her coworkers, but even I could tell she was bored.

Everybody who needed medical attention mattered, but I knew my friend. She craved a challenge, and the facts were that the difficult cases, the *interesting* cases, and the fast paced environment were located right in the heart of the city, at University hospital.

"We'll see," she insisted, brushing her hair aside to show her pretty honey-toned face. A spattering of light brown freckles covered her nose and fanned onto her high cheekbones, a trait she'd inherited from her mother, who was *my* mother's bestie. Devyn was two years older than me, but she didn't feel like a big sister. She felt like my *twin.*

"Okay, okay." I tried to tone down my beaming smile. "I'll leave you alone I guess, since you're all embarrassed now."

"Uh huh. Let's talk about something else… like the college cutie you got in trouble about."

"*Ugggh,*" I groaned. "Let me guess – Imara and Irene have been bumping gums."

Devyn giggled. "You already know it. Now, last *I* heard, J. Wright had you ready to toss your panties at him. Now you're verbally sparring with this kid?"

"He's not a kid," I corrected quickly. "He's your age, a grown ass man. And he *still* has me ready to toss my panties at him."

"Ooooh!" Her eyes lit up. "That means goodbye

Grayson, right?"

I sucked my teeth. "Wrong. This Jason thing is all hypotheticals and scenarios that'll never happen. My boyfriend is Grayson."

"So the rhyming is just a coincidence?"

"Uhh, *yes*," I laughed. "I know you don't like

Gray, but—"

"Girl *you* don't even like him," Devyn quipped, wrinkling her nose. "He's not even your type. He's all… *gray*."

I bit my lip to keep from laughing. Partially at the look on her face, partially because I understood exactly what she meant when she called him gray. Meaning neutral. Meaning *boring*. And maybe that was kinda why he worked for me.

Grayson was a very buttoned-up type of guy. Nice job as a young lawyer, nice condo downtown, nice looking… just... nice. No chance of me getting too wrapped up in our relationship, when the only thing I was trying to be wrapped up in right now was securing my education and career, since I was already two years behind.

He was perfect.

"He's my type *for now*. And neither of us is thinking long term, so it's not like that's a big deal."

"It's a big waste of time though."

I was opening my mouth to offer a weak response when the doorbell rang, and I hopped right up to answer. "Saved by the bell," Devyn called after me, and I grinned as I reached for the deadbolt, putting my eye up to the peephole before I disengaged the lock.

Shit!

"It's mama!" I whisper-yelled to Deyvn, stepping back into the living room. Her eyes went wide in confusion, and I motioned toward our pizza and wing boxes, and the pouches from our store-bought frozen cocktails.

"Ohhh, shit!"

Devyn immediately went to work, gathering and

everything and running with it into the kitchen. I couldn't do anything about the smell of pizza and liquor that was probably on my breath, but I unbolted and opened the door anyway.

"Hey mama!"

She breezed past me into my living room, just as Devyn stepped in from the kitchen.

"Daaang Auntie!" she said, making a circle around my mother as she posed, shoulders back, head held high. "Why are you all dressed up like this?"

"Out being fast," I said, grinning as I came to stand beside Devyn. My mother was wearing a flirty, leopard print circle skirt that skimmed her thighs, a sleeveless silk blouse, and sky-high heeled sandals. She'd looked amazing when she left, but now, she had a little glow of happiness all over her face.

She shot me a censoring look, even though she blushed. "I was not out being fast, I was asked on a date."

"Why is all your lipstick gone if you weren't being fast?"

"Why does your place smell like pizza and hot wings?" She lifted an eyebrow.

My mouth dropped open. "Umm… so what you're saying is that we should both mind our business, huh?"

"Mmhmm."

"Message received."

Devyn shook her head, laughing. "Y'all are a trip. What does he look like?"

"You know who Henry Simmons is, right?" I chimed in before my mother could answer. "From NYPD Blue? Imagine him a couple shades darker, about sixty years old, with a little salt and pepper thing going on."

"Damn," Devyn said. "Go ahead then, Auntie!"

Our laughter was interrupted by the doorbell again, and I stepped away to answer.

Shit, I thought, as soon as my silly ass opened the door without looking and saw the deliveryman on the other side.

"*More* hot wings Reesie?"

I cringed as my mother's voice rang from behind me, but didn't turn around as I collected my food and paid. When I turned around, Devyn had walked up too, and immediately took the Styrofoam carton from my hands.

"Thank you for ordering these for me twinnie," she said, winking at me as she grabbed her keys and purse from the hook. "My liquor has worn off, so I'm going to head out, y'all have fun, nice to see you Auntie, bye!"

Her words came out as one long sentence as that heifer snuck off, after conning me out of my wings. I couldn't even argue the point in front of my health-nut mother either, cause we were *both* supposed to be on this low-fat, low-sodium, low-yumminess kick before what I referred to as comfort-food season started.

"You're coming running with me in the morning, right?"

I sighed, then closed the door behind Devyn.

"Don't I always?"

"You sound really enthusiastic, my dear," she quipped, shaking her head. "And yet, you always claim to feel great afterward."

That was true. I complained and acted like I was dying before and during every early-morning run, but I unfailingly felt amazing after, even if it was early as hell in the morning. Her yoga habit was the same situation.

I pushed a sugary smile to my face. "Yaaay? Is that better?" I asked, my fake smile turning into a real one when she scowled. "So… are you going to tell me about your date? Did you have a good time? Did he kiss you?"

She lifted an eyebrow as a smile tugged the corners of her mouth. "He took me to listen to jazz and have dinner, and it was lovely. I had a wonderful time.

And I don't kiss and tell… my daughter. I'm *not* telling you."

"Oh booo! Why did you come by then?"

She settled into a seat on the couch and took off her shoes. "To find out how your apology to Jason

Wright went."

I giggled. "It went well."

"Uh huh. Then why are you laughing?"

"Ohh, no reason. Don't worry mama. I didn't say anything he'll be able to complain about." I'd made sure of *that*.

Oh, I'd apologized all right, but did it in such a way that even my apology was insulting. Of course I knew his feelings weren't really hurt – we were playing chess. And in my probably biased opinion, I was kicking his ass. Of course I knew he wasn't trying to get me in trouble – he was forcing me to engage with him. And I'd even crushed *that* by making it clear that I wouldn't.

If Mr. Wright wanted to play with me, he was going to have to pull his best moves out.

five.

JASON

So Professor Bryant bought herself a new whip.

Luxury cars didn't come through our service center too often, so the sleek black beauty definitely caught my eye. She only wanted minor changes on the trim package – a different set of rims, modified console, things like that, but we had to order a few parts, so all in all, it took a week to get her car ready.

And of course *I* got the job of dropping it off.

I wondered if she knew J&P was my father's place? The logo on the sleeve of the mechanic's shirt I wore sometimes was tiny, and it was one of the biggest – and only black owned – dealerships in the city. It made sense that she *wouldn't* have known, at least initially, but what about now?

Is that why he sent me to drop off this car?

I groaned.

I'd made the mistake of lamenting that grade out loud to him and my brother's at dinner last Sunday… was this his way of trying to help me out? Curry some favor with the professor for a better grade next time?

At that, I chuckled.

That wasn't my father's style.

But, I did notice that he wasn't dropping the car off himself, even though his name was listed as the salesman on the paperwork.

Hmmm.

Professor Bryant was around the same age as my father, and she was fine as hell. Even when he wasn't on the market to date, my father had never been one to turn down a chance to do a little respectful flirting with a pretty woman. The only reason I could think of that Pops wouldn't do this delivery himself was to avoid getting himself in trouble with his mystery woman.

Ha.

Smart man.

In any case, it was because of this drop off that instead of spending my Saturday morning with an engine, I was reluctantly in khakis and the corny J&P polo, driving Professor Bryant's car to her house. One of the other guys from the service center was with me, trailing me in another car so I could get back to the dealership after the drop off. Plus, my official capacity today was salesman, which I hated, so if there were any adjustments needed, or problems with the car, I was supposed to let him handle it.

Like that was actually going to happen.

In any case, I pulled up in front of this perfectly manicured modern craftsman style house. There was a big driveway that even led to the back of the house, so I took advantage of the space by parking it in a way that the car would look especially good from the front door. Or at least I tried. There was a little annoying dark purple Audi parked right in my sight line, and I frowned at it.

Didn't seem like something the professor would drive.

I did one last little inspection over the car, making sure everything looked perfect before I ambled up to the front door. The big front window was wide open, blinds, curtains, and all, and I could hear music blasting from inside – chicks singing and rapping about "feeling themselves". I couldn't really see anything except a deep purple couch that separated the living room from the kitchen, but I recognized the strong lavender scent of purple fabuloso cleaning products. My mother had used the same thing, but damn… what was with all the purple?

I rang the doorbell once, and then a second time when minutes passed and nobody came to the door. Thankfully the song ended, and I hurriedly pushed the doorbell again in the break in the music.

A couple of seconds later, the door swung open, and the purple *everything* suddenly made sense.

"What the hell do *you* want?" Reese asked, leaning on the mop she'd brought with her to the front door. I wanted to come back with a snarky response, but I was distracted by pretty copper skin. Lots and lots of skin.

She'd come to the door in a gray sports bra that was doing an admirable job of trying to keep her contained. The matching gray shorts she wore came down to mid-thigh, yeah, but they were lycra, or something else, that fit tight against her skin. I wasn't trying to always find myself ogling her like this, but *goddamn.*

"Can I help you?" she snapped, and I ran my tongue over my lips before I unhurriedly brought my gaze up to her face. She was pissed, and I almost wanted to laugh, because I don't think she realized that *pissed* was sexy as hell on her.

Big browns narrowed, plush lips twisted into a frown. I had the strongest urge to grab her by the high ponytail she'd pulled her braids into and kiss her, and watch that little attitude melt away, but I was on official

business... and I wouldn't put it past Reese to pull out a blade. What the hell was she doing here anyway, with a mop? Damn, did Professor B make her grad assistant clean her house too?

Ahhh, maybe this is more of her punishment from that email... God I hope so.

She cleared her throat, and let the mop lean in the doorway as she crossed her arms, waiting for me to explain my presence.

"I'm looking for Professor – I mean, Imara Bryant."

"She's not here."

Motherfucking déjà vu.

Internally, I sighed, then nodded. "Okay. When will she be back?"

"I have no idea."

"You never have useful information, do you? You work here and don't know when the owner is going to be back?"

She sucked her teeth, her face twisting into a deeper scowl. "*Work here*?! Boy this is *my* house. Excuse you."

"What? So you live with the professor?"

"I *live* alone."

"Then why is this address on the paperwork?"

"Because it's a duplex," she snapped, then jabbed a finger toward my chest. "*You* need to drive around back."

I blew out a heavy sigh, then took a step back.

"You couldn't have just said that in the first place?"

She smirked. "What was it that you said that day in the office? *That's not even what you asked me*."

I narrowed my eyes, and nodded. "Aiight. Got it." Shaking my head, I stepped down off the porch and climbed back into the car. I hadn't driven two feet before Reese came outside and waved me down.

She'd slid some thonged sandals on, but hadn't put on any more clothes, and in the full sunlight… again, *goddamn*. She walked right up to the car, when I let the window down she leaned, dropping her head so we were face to face.

"Oh yeah," she said. "She's not at home. Your little paperwork should say somewhere that you're authorized to drop the car off with me."

I put a hand to my forehead, squeezing to relieve some frustration and pressure. This girl was trying to stress me to death – only possible explanation. I turned the car off and climbed out, leaving the door open for her

to look around inside, but she didn't move back. Instead, we ended up rounding each other, looking each other up and down.

“Nice khakis,” she said, once she was the one closest to the car, and then turned to look at it.

I looked at it too – not the car. Reese was on the slimmer side of curvy, fit, but still nice and soft. And her *ass…* perfect upside-down heart over toned thighs, just a couple inches from my hands.

Well within grabbing distance.

She put her knees on the front seat, bending over into the passenger side to examine something. I stuck my hands in my pockets, and was still talking myself into looking away from those twin dimples on her back when she turned around. First, her eyes cut over to her ass, then up to me, glaring at me over her shoulder.

“Could you take a step back? My boyfriend would kill you if he saw you looking at me like that.”

I laughed. “If your boyfriend was hitting it right, I doubt I’d *be* looking at you like this. You’d have a much better disposition.”

“My man is *hitting it* just fine, asshole.”

Again, I had to laugh. “Yeah, whatever you need to say to convince yourself he ain’t wack. As a matter of fact, I don’t believe you have a man that would put up with you.”

She scoffed as she backed out of the car, and I *did* step away to give her some room, or her ass would have been against my dick. She got right in my face, smelling like fabuloso, and crossed her arms.

“You realize that doesn’t quite ring true when it’s obvious your ass can’t resist me, right?”

I lifted an eyebrow. "Can't resist you? Woman… I'd ask if you were crazy, but I already know the answer to that."

"So I'm crazy now? I haven't been that crazy when you couldn't keep your eyes off me. And I bet I'm not that crazy when you're thinking about how you're going to fabricate another interaction with me."

"*I'm* fabricating interactions?" – that was true, but whatever – "What about you *purposely* picking fights?"

She smirked. "I haven't picked any fights with you – I just haven't backed down from them. I can see why you'd be confused about that though."

I tossed my head back, letting out a shout of laughter. "I swear, you are the most irritating, abrasive, snarky woman I've ever met."

Reese stepped in a little closer, barely leaving any space between us as she looked up into my eyes. "And that's *exactly* why you want me so bad, isn't it?" *Yes. Hell yes.*

But of course I didn't *say* that.

"I'm not into evil princesses with nasty attitudes, no matter how good they look."

"And I'm not into arrogant mechanics with sticks up their asses." She cocked an eyebrow. "So where exactly do we go from here?"

Before either of us could say anything else, I heard someone call her name from over my shoulder. I

glanced back to see a car I hadn't even heard pull up, a silver Lexus with chrome trimmings. Nice.

Standing on the other side of it was one of those corporate type of dudes that I had – correctly, apparently

– pegged as Reese's type. He stepped from behind the car, cautiously, wearing khakis on purpose, looking between me and Reese like he was considering a call to the police. He called her name again, still cautious, damn near high-pitched, and I didn't even bother trying to hide my derisive smirk as I turned back to her.

"*This* is the nigga that was going to "kill me" over you?" I chuckled, shaking my head. Her nostrils flared as she scowled at me, hard, but her lack of denial answered my question. "Hey, listen…" I dropped my head toward her, speaking into her ear. "You ever need somebody to hit it *right*… you let me know. Aiight?"

"Reese, are you okay?"

I rolled my eyes. Here this dude was, creeping up like he couldn't see the big J&P Auto logo on my chest.

"I'm fine, Gray," Reese said, stepping around me. His eyes bulged out when he saw how she was dressed, but I doubt she cared. "He's from the dealership. He was just here dropping my mother's car off. And now he's about to go."

Mother?!

I narrowed my eyes, looking at Reese's face. If I squinted a little, and imagined her with designer glasses

like Professor B always wore to class… damn. I could see the resemblance.

Reese held out her hand, and I dropped the keys into it. "You have a nice day ma'am," I said, then turned to walk to the other car, where my coworker was waiting.

"Oh!" I turned back, and "Gray" was already in her face, looking like he was about to get cursed out. They both looked up, and I winked at Reese. "Don't forget my offer."

"What offer? What offer is he talking about?"

"Relax," I snapped, closing my fist around the keys Jason had dropped into my hand. "He's a car salesman, just talking about some deal."

It probably wasn't fair to Grayson to be so annoyed with him, but I was *seething* mad. Mad as hell that Jay's offer had turned me on so much. Mad as hell that Grayson had shown up unannounced, looking all… not at all like the type who would kick somebody's ass about their girlfriend.

Mostly because he wouldn't.

Mostly because I was barely his girlfriend.

I hadn't seen – and had barely heard – from him in the over two weeks since the night I'd passed up Refill with Olivia to kick it with him. And we hadn't even kicked it, not really. He'd pawed at me a few times until I gave him some ass, and then he promptly fell asleep.

I woke him up and sent him home.

Generally speaking, I wasn't that bothered. I didn't really have the time or energy for a boyfriend anyway, I just needed convenient companionship, and

Grayson fit the bill. Honestly, it hadn't started out like that. When we met, we were really into each other, if for nothing other than shallow reasons.

He was all shiny and pretty, with thick black curls he kept cut low, and creamy caramel skin, and sexy light brown eyes. Tall, and decently built, with an easy laugh. Just pretentious enough with his law degree and his

Lexus and his standing lunch date with the Mayor's office to appeal to my slightly pretentious nature. He was busy, I was busy, and his dick was big, so it was the perfect scenario for a casual, shallow relationship that was about 65% sex, 35% actually liking each other. I wasn't the jealous type by any means – I pushed for exclusivity for my health. I wasn't about to fight anybody over him, or end up with a disease.

We'd been seeing each other for almost two years, and I used to get so excited about our time together. He treated me like he was lucky to have me, sending flowers, random texts, and offering up sweet, passionate sex when we were able to make our schedules mesh.

Over the last six months though, that had stopped.

He got even busier, trying to make partner at his law firm, and so did I, after accepting the grad assistant position officially. I didn't really miss the flowers, but the loss of the sentiment stung. I *did* miss the silly texts he used to send, and while sweet sex wasn't what I wanted all the time, I definitely missed the fact that he used to make an effort, because now he just didn't. Like last week.

And now he popped his Al B. Sure! looking ass up at the most inopportune time, with the nerve to act like he had a problem. I was always pretty mellow with him – he didn't bring out the slick mouth that Jason did – but *whew*… I was two seconds off of cursing him out. "Yeah, with you wearing *that*? Sure, I'm sure he was incredibly interested in talking to you about low interest rate car loans. What, did he want to take you for a

"ride"?"

I sucked in a deep breath, and then counted to ten before I opened my mouth. "I was cleaning, and planning to go for a run when I was done. I'm wearing workout clothes, not a G-string and bikini top. And let's be clear – if I *was* wearing that, it would be my prerogative, because

I'm a grown ass woman, and I'll wear what I want."

"I-I'm just saying, damn. How am I supposed to feel when this big buff dude was towering over you, looking at you like he wanted to snatch you up?"

I suppressed a shiver from running up my spine at the thought of Jason "snatching me up". Gray made it sound like a bad thing… but I guess to him it probably was. The thing was though, if he had a problem, why didn't he straighten up his damn back, and walk over with confidence? Ask what was going on? Palm my booty to make it clear I was his?

Instead, he slunk over from behind his car, eyeing the army tattoos on Jason's broad arms. With his hand in his pocket, no doubt unlocking his phone in case he needed to summon the police. Calling my name with no bass in his voice, like he expected *me* to do the claiming and protecting.

I wasn't nearly progressive enough for *that* shit. I let out a heavy sigh.

"I get it," I said, trying not to flinch when he pulled me into an embrace. The lack of warmth I felt made it clear to me that our relationship ship was well past the climax, and reaching the resolution. Fast. It just wasn't a conversation I was ready to have today.

"What are you even doing here?" I asked. "I thought you had some legal conference or something to get to today?"

He gave me a beautiful smile that did nothing for me, moving his hands to grab handfuls of my ass and

squeeze. "I do, this afternoon. But I was hoping that before I drove up there, you could give me a nice little send off..."

I'm not quite sure how I controlled myself from sneering. "Um, let's raincheck, okay? I wish you'd called. I really have to finish my weekly cleaning, and I have to get this run in, and-"

"So you'd rather clean, and work out, than be with me?" His hands loosened their hold on me, and he stepped away, shaking his head. "Or is this about the little stare off between you and GI Joe?"

"Oh *God*," I rolled my eyes. "No. I'm just not feeling it right now. Is that a crime?"

"Not feeling *it*, or not feeling *me*?"

I bit my lip. I was trying so hard but…

"You know what? Not feeling *you.* You claim you're too busy to even send me a damned text message throughout the day, and the first time you get to see me in two weeks, you want to drop by for a quickie? Really

Gray? That seemed like a good plan to you?"

He opened and closed his mouth for a few seconds, like he was searching for something to say, before he finally dropped his shoulders. "I thought that's what you would want?" he said weakly, and I bit down on my lip again as I nodded.

"Did you? Okay."

His face brightened. "Okay? So come inside, let's do this…"

I pushed his hand off my ass. "No, you misunderstood. We're not having sex today. If all you have time for is a quickie, you don't have time to make up for falling asleep after those five pumps last time I saw you, for not making any effort to talk to me these last few weeks, and the *months* before that, or for dropping by here unannounced like this is a cat house!"

He recoiled backwards. "Damn, Reesie… what has gotten into you? Why are you being so mean?" Mean?

Mean?

He looked damn near ready to cry, when Jason would have…*Ugh!*

I looked away from him, inhaling a deep breath through my nose, letting it stream out of my mouth before I brought my gaze back to his. "I'm sorry for being mean, but I think you should go ahead to your conference."

Not giving him a chance to respond, I climbed in my mother's car, moving it down to her driveway. I hoped that by the time I was done, Gray would have gotten the picture, and taken his ass home.

I stopped in my tracks as I headed into the library, narrowing my eyes at a familiar-looking car. I thought about it for a few seconds and then went in, heading straight for the second floor.

"Liv!" I called out, when I spotted her coming out of the bathroom, fixing her clothes. I could have sworn she saw me before I said her name, but maybe she was just distracted. She seemed flustered when she turned around, but her face bloomed into a bright smile as I approached.

"Hey, Reese! What are you doing here?"

I lifted an eyebrow. "Umm, it's the library… where the books are, and my mom's classroom, and office…"

"Ah! Right! Sorry." She shook her head, then finished smoothing her clothes. "I'm a little bit out of it."

"Girl, we all have our days. Hey, have you seen Gray in here?"

Her eyes went wide, and she leaned her head forward a little. "Who?"

I laughed. "Grayson… my boyfriend, crazy girl!"

Olivia and I hadn't known each other very long – just the past two years, since I'd started grad school. We weren't confidant-friends, more like "hey let's go out/do lunch", but she'd met Grayson before, on more than one occasion at Refill.

"Ohhh," she said, nodding. I shook my head. She really *was* out of it today. "Umm, yeah. Some hours ago, over in the legal section. He was researching case law."

"Oh." I twisted my mouth a little. "I thought all of that was available online?"

Olivia's face spread into a weak smile. "Oh, you know how Grayson is. Likes to put his hands on it. Touch the pages."

"So… he's up here often?"

"No, I wouldn't say often," she shook her head. "Has he not mentioned it to you? Is everything okay with you guys?"

"Of course," I lied with a smile. "Like I said, we all have our days, and I'm a little out of it myself. I'm gonna head on to this office. See you later."

She nodded. "Okay. Bye hon!"

I turned and walked away from Olivia, trying to keep my shoulders relaxed even though I was seething inside. Another a week and a half had passed with minimal contact between me and Grayson, though he had apologized for that stupid Saturday morning.

The thing was, I wasn't looking for an apology. I didn't want his meaningless words, I wanted him to *do* something. I wanted him to let me know he was going to be at the law library while I was on campus, I could help him research. I wanted him to send me those random messages again throughout the day. I wanted him to stop by my place in the middle of the night, wake me up, and screw me back to sleep. I wanted him to make me forget Jason Wright existed.

I wanted… something that wasn't the relationship we'd established.

But just like that Saturday morning we'd fought, I wasn't trying to think about that. I had other things on my mind. I had my *own* paper due next week, and a test, plus heavier shit that I was trying to ignore. Men weren't in the top five list of things I needed to be thinking about. Hell, they weren't even in the top ten, but somehow

Grayson's actions had sunk my already sullen mood even further.

As I turned the corner to get to my mother's office, I walked right into a tall, broad body. I was moving so fast that I damn near bounced backwards, but strong arms went around me, keeping me balanced.

"Sorry," I said, then stepped away, and was already about to continue my journey down the hall when he spoke up.

"That's it? No insult today?"

My head popped up, and I really looked at who

I'd bumped into.

Jason.

I hadn't seen him since last Saturday either, but he'd certainly been on my mind. I'd needed to meet with one of my professors during the time I would have normally seen him in my mother's class, and I felt halfway insane for almost… kind of… *missing* him.

Although we hadn't been in each other's presence, I'd read his words. The class was on the romance novel that I'd recommended to my mother, and the students had been tasked with giving their preliminary thoughts, at the halfway point of the book. Not a full paper, not even a critique, not about the technical aspects, not really. Just their casual thoughts.

"Honestly? I think these two are silly. I'll admit that I don't read a ton of romance novels, but does this dynamic ever work? According to his description of her, Vivienne is smart, sexy, successful, and amazing in bed according to these sex scenes. What man wouldn't want to make her his? Well, this idiotic one in this book,

Carter. I'm a little past halfway, and she just dropped the "what am

I to you?" bomb on him, and I swear I wanted to smack this dude for his reaction. If he wasn't into her like that, okay, I would get it.

But that's not the case. He ***loves*** *this girl, but instead of admitting that, and explaining whatever (most likely bullshit) reason he has to not be with her, he broke her heart. It's not cool. Not at all."*

I was supposed to be commenting on these. I was supposed to be asking questions, pulling more from them based on their thoughts, compiling a list that my mother would use to discuss love, romance, and dysfunctional family dynamics in literature. The next book on their list was literary fiction, with a heavy romance element. The one after that was more focused on families. They'd be contrasting the difference between how different elements were interwoven in the three novels.

So it was important. And still, I was putting it off. For one, because the class was still reading the book, and there was still time before that discussion. Also?

I wasn't sure I wanted to know what Jason's thoughts were on life, and love. I was intrigued enough without that.

"No, not today," I said, giving him a wry smile.

"Wow, do I need to check your temperature or something? Call a doctor?"

I laughed a little as I studied him, and shook my head. "Nah. Not necessary."

He was wearing the mechanic's shirt again today, and for the first time, I noticed the "*J. Wright*" embroidered above the pocket. No idea how I'd missed it before. "Okay," he said, nodding. It was almost funny, that he looked so genuinely confused. "You sure you're aiight?"

"Yes," I lied, for the second time in less than five minutes. "I'm fine."

"See you in class Friday?"

I smirked. "What, did you miss me or something?"

"Nah," he said, after sucking his teeth. "Nobody missed your mean ass. I just noticed you weren't there is all."

"Uh huh. Sure."

"You gonna answer the question?"

I let out a little sigh, then brought my gaze up to meet his, forcing myself to smile. "I… don't know yet. I *never* know useful information. Remember?" I winked at him, and then turned away, finishing my trip down the hall to my mother's office.

That little flirting had stripped the last of my emotional energy, and I unlocked the door with what felt like the last of my physical too. I closed it behind me, and then dropped into the chair at the desk I used, resting my head on the desk with a sigh.

After a few moments had passed, I pulled out my phone, navigating it to a particular number. I waffled for several moments, knowing I couldn't call it, but wanting to anyway. Finally, I tucked it away. Pulled out my laptop, started it up, and dove into my work.

Anything to absorb myself in and make it through the next few days.

six.

I didn't make it to class Friday.

Not my class, not my mother's class, and I didn't even bother explaining, because she already knew why. I slept in as late as my body would let me – nine in the morning, even after I'd been up at midnight the night before to go for a run.

As soon as the sunlight pulled me from my sleep, I got up, drank a cup of Valerian tea, took more melatonin, and climbed my ass right back in the bed to toss and turn. By the time 2pm rolled around, it was clear that my body wasn't on board with my idea to sleep away the cognizance that this day even existed.

Logic said that a bottle of wine would easily solve my problem, but I wasn't interested in dealing with the hangover after. Instead, I pulled myself out of bed and showered until the water ran cold, and I had to get out.

2:42.

I pulled an oversized tee-shirt over my head and made my way into the kitchen, searching for something that would spark an appetite. Almond milk, wheat bread, special K, tomatoes, rice crackers, apples, dried lentils, chicken breast… I pushed out a heavy sigh. Nobody wanted any of that shit.

I let the refrigerator swing closed, and then just stood there, looking… crazy. Another heavy sigh, and I made my way into the living room, grabbing the remote before I flopped down on the couch. I'd just turned the TV on when my doorbell rang, and I debated about whether or not I planned to answer. It sounded again, with a little more urgency, and I drug myself up from the couch to get it.

The same delivery guy from a few weeks ago stood on my doorstep, holding what I *knew* were Thai spicy wings, even through the closed box. That sweet, piquant aroma drifted up to my nose, making my stomach rumble with hunger. I didn't even know the circumstances – I just thanked God for provision, and signed the little slip confirming I'd gotten them. He waved me off when I said I had to grab my wallet, telling me the bill was already paid.

I lit into that box before the door was even closed, licking sticky red-brown sauce from my fingers as I kicked it shut. I stood there in my foyer eating, and was through half of the set of ten wings when I figured I should probably see which one of my love ones had rescued me.

My cell phone was off, and had been all morning. I hadn't planned to turn it on at all today, but it probably wasn't the best idea in the world to be completely unavailable. As soon as it powered on, it began pinging and vibrating, informing me of social media notifications and new texts.

There were a couple from my mother, which I immediately returned, because I didn't want her worrying about me. Same with Devyn, who was at work now, but had sent me a picture of herself with a box of wings, captioned ***"Twin with me boo! I know Auntie makes you keep all that health-nut stuff in the house, but I had a feeling you might need something a little different***

today. Let me know if you need me. *hugs*"

I smiled. Of course my bestie had thought to take care of me. I sent her a message back as well, thanking her for the wings and assuring her that I was fine, even if it wasn't completely true. She didn't get off from her shift at the hospital until two in the morning and I didn't want *her* worrying about me either.

The last message surprised me.

"Dani Renee at Refill tonight… you wanna go? – Grayson" Hmm.

I still hadn't said anything about him being at the library and not bothering to try to see me, because we hadn't been in touch. He'd been busy doing whatever the hell he was doing, and I was busy trying not to have an emotional breakdown. But really, I wasn't even interested anymore. Once I was past my funk, I would make it official, but we were so far past the expiration date that our milk was turning to yogurt.

"No, sorry. Not in the mood."

"No surprise there. – Grayson."

I tilted my head to the side, staring at my phone, because what the whole entire fuck? No "hey, what's wrong?" or "do you need anything?", just a smart ass remark. Even Jason's rude ass had the decency to ask what was going on with me when he could tell I wasn't myself, but not the guy that was supposed to be my boyfriend?

I dropped the phone in my lap, disgusted, and picked up the rest of my wings. A few minutes later, I went and opened that wine, pouring half down the drain to make sure I didn't drink it. Back at the couch, I realized just how intuitive that was. I turned the bottle back, and didn't let it down until half of what was left was gone.

I finished my wings, finished my wine, and about an hour later, I was passed out sleep again in front of the TV.

- & - I woke up with a jolt.

My mouth was dry, and the tiniest hint of a headache was needling into my brain until I sat up, and life began to flow back into my limbs. I felt groggy, but through the fog, I realized that Dani Renee, a pretty neosoul singer known for her haunting voice and red locs, was on my TV. She was giving an interview, but as I watched, it cut to a clip from one of her shows. Her distinctive voice sliced right through my morose attitude, hitting me in the gut, and I knew right then that yeah… I *was* going to Refill tonight.

Fuck Grayson.

I texted mama and Devyn where I would be, and then turned the TV off and hooked my phone to my sound system, blasting Dani's CD as I took another shower. Summer was cooling into fall, so I had a perfect excuse to wear the cute combat boots I'd purchased on sale back in June, paired with a short, flowy pink longsleeved dress that hung off my shoulders.

My phone chimed, and I checked it, noticing a message from Olivia, asking if I was going to Refill tonight. I already knew *she* was, because she *always* was, so I didn't even bother responding. I'd see her when I got there tonight.

I pulled my braids back from my face and secured them with a clip, then brought some of them forward over one shoulder. I put on the biggest hoop earrings I had, plus some bracelets and the engraved nameplate necklace I never left home without. Some bb cream, liner, mascara, and a little lipstick, and I… still felt like shit.

I'd slept for damn near five hours after my wings and wine, so it was already nine at night before I left my house. I climbed into my little purple Audi and made my way across town, fighting the Friday night crowds to find a place to park.

I had to walk a bit to get to Refill, but the vibrant energy of the city was doing me some good. No matter how much I wanted to stay home and sleep the day away, now that I was out, I actually did feel better. It was nearing ten o clock by the time I made it into Refill, and the dynamic was beyond hype inside. According to the bartender, Dani was taking a little break but would be back on stage in a few minutes. I ordered a cranberry vodka and sprite, and sipped it while I walked around, looking for familiar faces.

It didn't take me long to find one.

I saw Olivia, sitting down at one of the elevated bar-height tables along the perimeter of the club. The room was dark, brightened every few moments by the flash of a strobe light, but those tables each had a little individual spotlight, thanks to the sconces on the wall.

She was grinning hard as hell – smiling bigger than I'd *ever* seen. As much as she came out, Olivia wasn't really a party girl. She forced herself to do it to be seen. When we first met, I'd had to drag her out after one too many complaints about being bored with just doing work and school. She'd attached herself to me – going out when I did, getting her nails done at the same place, shopping where I did. She took that little push I'd given her and ran with it – hell, she even dressed better than me now. I didn't mind it, but it bugged the shit out of Devyn. I just saw it as her blossoming.

And blossom, she *had.*

Her grown ass had been painfully shy about men when we met, but now here she was, half-shrouded in shadows, giggly pleasure illuminated on her face while some dude whispered in her ear and kissed on her neck.

In public.

I shook my head, even though the sight brought about one of the very few smiles I'd been able to summon today. Student had unquestionably surpassed the master, because I was nowhere near bold enough for that.

I kept sipping from my drink as I weaved my way to her through the crowd. The emcee announced that Dani was about to get on the stage, and I wanted to be front and center for that. I could say hi to Liv first though.

"Olivia!" I called over the din of the crowd when I was a couple of feet away, and realized there was a rail separating me from the area with the tables. I would have to walk around to a short staircase to get to where she was. She looked up, and I waved, then wiggled my eyebrows at her as I cut my eyes toward the guy she was with, who was apparently a vampire and trying to suck her damn neck off.

Her eyes went wide when they landed on me, and I giggled, and nodded. "*Busted*!" I mouthed at her, and laughed. "Fast ass!"

That crazy wide eyed look still hadn't left her face, but she slid her eyes away from mine and over to her new boy toy. Her lips moved – she said something, but not to me, and just as Dani Renee's band played their first notes, he detached himself from her neck, turned around, and looked me right in the face.

My smile died on my lips, and I hopped that fucking railing with my drink still in my hand. "Well this is *cozy*." I stopped right in front of the table, looking back and forth between her and Grayson.

"When exactly did this happen?"

"When you decided to stop being a good gir—"

"Shut the hell up," I snapped at Grayson, who'd taken it upon himself to answer a question that wasn't directed at him. "I'm not talking to you. *Fuck you.* I'm talking to the bitch that's supposed to be my friend."

I turned my scowl back to Olivia, who looked like she wanted to crawl in a hole and die. At that moment, I wanted that for her too.

"Reesie, I—"

"Don't call me *Reesie*. Friends call me Reesie. It's

Reese for you."

She swallowed hard, her eyes darting around like she was looking for an escape. "Okay. Okay. I… um… I didn't mean for this to happen, I'm sorry! He just started coming to the library after you introduced us, and… and… "

"And *what*? You slipped and fell on his dick?

Come the hell on, Olivia! I mean… I know we aren't *best* friends, but come on! I've never been anything but cool with you, and you do *this*?"

"Why are you so mad?" Grayson drawled, and when I looked over at him, he was wearing a dumbass smirk. "You barely wanted me anymore anyway.

Consider this moving on… no harm done."

"No harm done?! You could have given me something from this… *ugh!*"

I took a deep breath, calming myself from screaming for everyone to hear that Olivia had screwed a good 10% of the male population in our city. For one, she was within her rights to screw whatever *single* men she wanted. For two, that was her business, and unlike her, I wasn't a grimy enough bitch to spread her information just because I was pissed.

Directing my voice at Grayson, I sneered. "Your corny ass better hope like hell that *no harm done* is true."

He chuckled. "Your prissy ass isn't going to do anything."

"Keep thinking that," I nodded, giving him an ugly smile, and then turned back to Olivia. "Let me give you one last little tip - I hope you don't think you won some sort of prize with this fool. He did this shit to me?

He'll do the same to you."

Finding the nerve from somewhere to get an attitude, Olivia scoffed. "But I'm not *you* Reese. You taught me some stuff, yeah, but you can't teach what you don't know… how to keep your man. I'm good."

On the other side of her, Grayson laughed, and in front of me, a sly grin crept onto Olivia's face. Behind me, the emcee announced the end of Dani's set, and the realization hit me that I'd missed the whole reason I came out. On today, of all days.

And these jackasses thought it was funny.

Okay.

I glanced down at my half-finished drink, then back up at Olivia. I'd watched plenty of trash reality TV in my free time, and seen those women act up. Enough to think that a drink to a woman's face because you were upset was a silly thing to do.

So I threw it in Grayson's stupid, smirking face instead. And while he was coughing and sputtering and cursing about the soda and alcohol burning his eyes, I slammed the glass down on the table, turned to a shocked Olivia, and yanked the bar stool right from under her legs, sending her crashing to the floor.

Now, I had the barstool in my hands. I didn't *plan* to do anything with it except put it down, but somebody must have thought different because it was snatched away. A few seconds later, big arms were gripping me from behind, dragging me away from the scene while I wriggled and fought.

"What the *hell* are you doing?!" A familiar voice demanded.

I was put back on my feet in the crowded back parking lot of the club, and turned to see Devyn's brother, Eric, standing behind me with an exasperated scowl. He worked security for Refill, and we playfully called him

"Big E." Because, well… he was big. He was also a teddy bear, but he tucked that away here, because this was work. Here, he wasn't allowing any nonsense to go down.

"Fighting again, Reesie? Is that what's happening, we're going back to that now?"

"*No,* Eric I just—"

"Just what?"

"I wasn't *fighting*—"

"It *looked* like fighting, the way you laid that girl on her ass, and looked like you were about to knock her head in. You're lucky I'd already spotted you, or no telling what-"

"There's plenty of telling what!" I screamed, and Eric stopped, putting his hands on his waist. "I'm telling you now, I wasn't about to do anything to her! I mean… yeah, I threw the drink in his face, and yanked the stool out, but that's all. And I'm not sorry. I hope her ass bone is sore as fuck tomorrow."

"Reesie," Eric scolded, even though he was trying not to laugh. "That's still not okay. They could press charges, and you've worked too hard to get back on track for some bullshit to mess up your life. Right?"

I swallowed hard. "Right."

He pulled me into a hug, and I settled into his arms. He easily enveloped me in his large frame, squeezing me tight. "I know this time of year is hard for you, but… come on. Don't self-destruct, aiight?"

I nodded as he let me go, trying my best to blink back tears.

"You're lucky this happened where it did, so you didn't have a big audience and make a scene. I'm gonna go back inside, talk to my people, see about smoothing this over. You… go home. *Now.*"

I let out a deep breath as he went back inside. That little half of a drink had definitely worn off, and now the little bit of a happy vibe I'd been building was completely gone, and I felt like shit.

I *shouldn't* have done that.

It *wasn't* cool.

But… a little smile crept onto my face at the memory of Olivia's expression as she fell off that stool. She *definitely* hadn't expected me to do that, while she wanted to play smug about screwing my boyfriend. It didn't matter if I didn't want him – he was mine until we broke up, officially. I was actually madder at her than I was at Grayson, because you weren't supposed to do your home girls like that. If it was just some random chick, whatever. But she knew damn well we were together, had asked me about him and all.

I shook my head.

That was probably why she was conveniently clueless the other day. Grayson wasn't going up there to study law. More like anatomy. *Hers.*

Oh, and I was pissed at him too. This city was huge – he could have chosen someone else. Or no one else, until he broke up with me because he wasn't feeling it, because that was what adults with decency did.

You sure weren't thinking about decency when you were flirting with and – literally – showing Jason Wright your ass.

I stopped in my tracks as I headed down the sidewalk, passing droves of people out to have a good time on Friday night. That was certainly true – I hadn't been thinking about anything but getting a reaction out of Jason. When I was around him, Gray barely even crossed my mind… but intuition told me he and Olivia had been screwing around long before *my* eyes started to wander. Not that multiple wrongs meant taking a left made sense, but it certainly made me feel less guilty about it.

But overall… screw both of them. I didn't need either of those trash bags in my life.

My stomach rumbled a little as I made my way back to my car, and instead of heading back to where I was parked, I went the other direction. The streets got a little emptier, buildings got a little older, people outside got a little more… hood. But that was alright.

I knew exactly where I was going.

seven.

JASON

I grinned as soon as I walked into Sammy's BBQ and bar, inhaling the smoky aroma – a blend of cigars, swishers, and the smoker out back where they prepared the best damned ribs this city had. For a long time, I hadn't been allowed to come to Sammy's, specifically because of the "bar" part. My dad would bring the food home to us, but it was well after I was grown that I actually stepped foot inside when it was occupied at night.

Sammy, the namesake and owner, was standing at a table just beyond the entrance, laughing with a group of guys playing poker. I spoke to a couple of people I knew, but hadn't seen in a while, as I approached, and then tapped him on the shoulder. He turned with a pleasant grin, probably thinking I was a just a regular patron with a question or something. As soon as recognition dawned on him, that grin turned into a big smile, and he pulled me into a hug.

"Jay Wright! If I ain't know better I'd think I'd seen a ghost. Where the hell you been?"

I stepped back, shaking his hand as he clapped me on the shoulder. "I been in the army, dude. I've been all over."

"Well I know *that*. I'm talking about since you been back. Your daddy told me two months ago you were coming home, but you shole ain't brought your ass down here to eat, catch up, nothing!"

I shook my head. "My bad, Sammy. Just been getting acclimated to a different lifestyle."

Sammy rolled his eyes. "*Acclimated*? Now see, that's the little fancy ass college coming out in you."

He and the whole table of poker players laughed at that, and I couldn't really do anything but laugh too. I knew it was nothing but love – Sammy drove my mother to the hospital to deliver me, with my brothers in tow.

That was back before the dealership was a thing, when my father was working late shifts, overnight to make sure we ate. Sammy was my father's friend, and damn near like an uncle to us. I would accept the little lightweight clowning with a good attitude – I should have come to see him sooner.

I stood there talking for a little bit longer, before a flash of something pink in my peripheral caught my attention. My eyes went a little wider, and I excused myself from Sammy to go investigate.

I was just about to walk away when Sammy caught my arm, a twinkle of amusement in his eyes.

"Proceed with caution, young buck. That one's a spitfire."

"Yeah," I replied. "I know."

She was sitting at the bar, nursing a glass of something dark. Her focus was so intense on the ice in her glass that she didn't even look up as I sat down. She knocked the rest of the drink back, and then motioned at the bartender for another.

"You've had enough," Lana told her, gently placing a glass of ice water on the worn, but wellpolished bar. "How you doing baby?" she said to me, smiling. Lana was Sammy's wife, and one of the first crushes I've ever had.

"I'm doing alright. Water for me too please."

She nodded. "Coming right up."

I turned to where Reese was sitting, and looked her over. Sammy's wasn't a dump by any means, but it was comfortable. It was worn, well broken-in. They made their business on people who stopped in to take out food, but the inside was for the neighborhood folks, honestly. It was the type of bar old heads came to play poker and smoke cigars. Reese was out of place.

"Nice boots," I said, leaning forward to see her face, partially obscured by her braids.

She turned toward me, just a little, enough to see that her eyes were red. "Thanks."

"Let me guess, trouble in paradise? Surprised to see you slumming on this end of town."

"Okay," she said – *slurred* – and then climbed off her barstool on obviously wobbly legs. "I'm not about to sit here and take shit from you, 'kay?"

"Yeah, I hear you princess," I said, standing up to catch her around the waist as she stumbled a little.

"Get your goddamn hands off me."

I shook my head. "I will, after I sit you back down. You're not clearheaded enough to be out in this neighborhood at night by yourself."

She sucked her teeth. "I'm not *stupid, Jason.* I wasn't leavin', I was goin' to the otha end of the bar to get away from you, stupid."

"You know each other Jay?" Lana asked from across the bar. "I was trying to monitor how much she had, and thought I cut her off at the right time… until she opened her mouth just now."

I chuckled. Reese sounded like she'd taken a muscle relaxer or something, and was having trouble moving her mouth.

"Yeah, I know her. Unfortunately." Reese mumbled something that sounded like *fuck you*, and I

shook my head again. "I'm gonna take her to sit down. Can you send two catfish baskets over to the table please?"

Lana smiled. "Sure will."

She cursed me out the whole way there, but I managed to wrangle Reese into a booth-style table. A waitress came by and I ordered more water, urging her to drink it, which she thankfully did. A couple minutes later, our food was dropped off.

"You eat catfish, right?" I asked, then popped a French fry into my mouth. "I know it's not salmon, or sushi, but this is how we do it around here."

She looked up at me with a sneer, but otherwise didn't respond. Instead, she grabbed the bottle of Louisiana hot sauce from the table, opened it, and loaded her food down before she began going in.

Guess that was my answer.

We ate in silence for several long minutes, and then finally, she spoke up. "You know I'm not *that* drunk, right?"

I lifted an eyebrow. "Could've fooled me."

She gave me a look, and then bit into a hushpuppy. "I'd barely eaten anything today. I'm definitely a little tipsy, but more than that… just hungry." I scoffed, but she did sound better already. And

I'd been hungry enough before to feel lightheaded and discombobulated, so maybe that made sense too. But still… I wasn't all the way convinced.

"So why were you drinking and crying? Was I right? Something happened with your little boyfriend?

Somebody was looking at you and he tried to kick their ass? You saw he wasn't worth shit?"

I was just messing around, trying to bait her into our normal dynamic, but she shook her head, knocking back a gulp of water. "No. Well, I *did* see that he wasn't shit, but I already knew that. Today was confirmation. Caught him with my frie—no. Caught him with a trollop

I *thought* was a friend."

"Trollop?" She shrugged, then savagely bit into a piece of heavily buttered Texas toast, and I chuckled.

"Man," I said. "You've got to admit that it's nice to be so privileged that a cheating boyfriend is the extent of your problems. That hit you so bad that you had to come to the regla' black folks side of town to drink."

Again… I was mostly just messing with her, but from the look on her face, she wanted to reach across the table and choke me. She finished chewing the bread in her mouth, then took a long sip from her glass before she fixed me with a glare.

"My father died today. Not like, *today*, but six years ago, today. It's not a fucking good day for me. I picked myself up, got out and did something, trying to cheer myself up. Trying to *forget*. So to find out today, of all days, about *that* shit? Yeah, I came to have a drink, okay?"

Shit.

"Reese, I—"

"These are my father's people! Sammy and Lana.

Lana was my father's cousin. They knew him, they know *me.* I came here to feel close to him, not to get fucking judged by you. Not today, *Jason.* Yeah, I got a little bougie in me, from my mother side of the family, but I've got a little "neighborhood" in me too. This is home, just as much as the campus side of town. I came to hurt around my family, not to "slum". So fuck you."

By the time she finished that little minimonologue, she had tears streaming down her face, and I felt like shit. It was clear that she'd been crying already when I walked in, from her eyes being red, but actually seeing her face wet made my damned chest hurt. Her tears turned to quiet sobs, and I started to slide out of the booth to try to comfort her, but she looked up with scowl.

"Stay your ass over there," she snapped. "I *don't* need you feeling sorry for me." She grabbed a handful of napkins from the dispenser on the table and cleaned her face, then pinned me with another glower. "They weren't gonna let anything happen to me. The only reason they even let you approach me or bring me over here, is because apparently, they know you too. But recognize – you're a family *friend*. I'm *family*."

"I see that now," I nodded, swallowing hard. "I was fucking with you Reese. I didn't mean anything by what I said. I get that you don't really feel like playing like that right now, though, so I'm sorry."

She sucked her teeth. "You should be. Come in here messing up my vibe." A few seconds of silence passed between us, and then she said, "But thank you."

I lifted an eyebrow. "For what?"

"For treating me to dinner."

"Who said I was treating?"

Reese stopped to frown at me, with a pickle slice halfway up to her mouth. "*I* said you were treating. It's just a fish basket. What, you can't afford a fish basket on a mechanic's salary? Do I need to pay for yours too? Is that why you're so testy, you can't afford a date?"

I drew my head back, and then opened my mouth, ready to light into her for that long list of wrong-ass assumptions, but then I caught a look at her face. Her expression was blank, but her eyes were smiling. "Aiight," I laughed. "Point taken. But, you were doing a little judging yourself, princess."

She shrugged, then wiped her hands on her napkin. "Yeah… I kinda was."

Silence again, while we ate, and then something occurred to me. "Hey… what did you do when you caught ol' boy messing around?"

Reese almost choked on her water, then shook her head. "You don't wanna know."

"The hell I don't, with a reaction like that!"

She pushed out a heavy sigh, playing with her

straw as she held her glass in front of her. "Umm… I threw a drink in his face, and snatched her seat from under her." She looked away as soon as those words were out of her mouth, and took a long sip of her water again, just before the waitress came by with refills.

My eyes were wide as hell as I waited for the server to leave, so I could hear more about that. I'd jokingly though that Reese might carry around a blade, but damn… was she *really* a little mini-thug?

"You did *what*?" I asked, as soon as we were alone again. "Are you serious?"

"I'm dead serious. And as wrong as I know it was… it felt good as hell."

I threw my head back and laughed. "Yeah, I bet it did. Wow, though."

"Mmmhmm."

I watched her for a few seconds as she played in the remnants of her fries. "Hey," – she looked up – "I almost expected you to tell me you pulled a Viv. Put on your sweats and got a bat, ready to go smash up his house."

Okay. So… I dropped a reference to the book I'd been reading for Professor B's class. The main female character,

Viv, had caught her boyfriend in some wild shit on social media, and was ready to risk it all for about five minutes before she thought better of it.

After those words left my mouth, Reese stared at me for a full five seconds, lips parted, before she dropped her gaze and let out a little sigh, smoothing her dress over her legs. I didn't even know what had compelled me to say some corny shit like that, but as I watched, a smile spread over her face. Even though she still wasn't looking at me, and was shaking her head like she didn't *want* to smile about it… mission accomplished.

She leaned forward onto the table, with her elbows propped on the laminate surface, and put her chin onto her hands. Something in the mood had shifted, yet again, and she looked up at me with those sexy big brown eyes.

"You remember that offer you made me?" she asked, and my whole damn mouth went dry.

I cleared my throat, and tried not to look like she'd snatched the wind out of my lungs with that question. I smirked. "Yeah. Why? You tryna take me up on it or something?"

"Yeah. Why not?"

Shit, she is killing me.

Almost any other night, under any other circumstances, I would already have her in my car right now after a statement like that. But on *this* night, she was tipsy, heartbroken, and mourning the death of her father… it wasn't really prime time for me to follow through.

"Because," I said, wetting my lips with my tongue. "You're not… you're not in any shape to be making a request like that."

"How do you figure?"

"Come on, Reese. You're not really yourself, right now."

"Come on, Jason—"

"Everybody calls me Jay."

"*Jason.* I hope you don't think you're doing some honorable thing right now – cause if you do, I'm about to tell you why that's bullshit."

I grinned, crossed my arms, and then sat back in my seat. "Okay. I'm listening."

"I'm cognizant enough to consent, I'm more pissed than hurt about the mess with Grayson, and regarding my father… this is the healthiest coping I've done in years. But besides *all* of that… I'm a grown woman. I'm capable of asking for what I need, when I need it. And what I need now, is the dick down you offered me two weeks ago. Or were you just making shit up, and that's not *really* something you can handle?"

I lifted an eyebrow, and then uncrossed my arms to give her a little round of applause. "Wow… that was compelling as hell, princess. But listen, Reese. I'm not one of these little nice dudes, who will take you home, wrap you up in a blanket and put you to sleep, like you really need. I'm also not going to "make love" to you. If that's what you really want, I'm not the guy. If you're asking me to take you home and fuck you, that's what

I'm gonna do."

She stared at me for a few seconds and the smiled, grabbing her purse from beside her.

"Great. Let's go."

eight.

What the heck are you doing Reesie?

Shaking my head at my reflection, I covered my face with the cool towel one more time, making sure I was completely calm.

Completely sober.

Completely *sure* I wanted to do this.

The ride from Sammy's had been quiet – I was sure Jason was mulling this over as hard as I was, because for all our shit talking, having sex with someone was a whole other level.

Especially when you end up in a relative stranger's house.

Yeah.

That.

I'd insisted that we come to his house instead of mine. The last thing I wanted was to have sex in a place where Gray had been, where I'd been with him.

Obviously I'd cleaned since the last time we were together, but just knowing that he'd been there at all made me want to scrub everything top to bottom, with bleach. That would happen before I even slept there again, so there definitely wasn't going to be any intimacy.

Not to mention, the memories. Gray and I used to have fun, and that was reflected in pictures on my dresser and mementos from things we'd done together. I didn't want to be anywhere near any of that.

So to Jason's place we came, with him driving.

I'd excused myself to the bathroom as soon as we got here, to see what I looked like after a bar fight, several drinks, and a ridiculous amount of crying. It wasn't good. I washed my face, dug a little miniature of mouthwash out of my purse to freshen my breath, and unpinned my braids to let them fall around my face. I used the bathroom, utilized my little packet of wipes to make sure everything was *extra* fresh, even though I'd showered right before I left my house. Went back and forth about it, and then decided to take my panties off and stash them in my purse. After a little debate, I took my strapless bra off too.

I was thinking about this too hard. Did men even care if you were extra fresh and pretty when they took you home from a BBQ joint?

I laughed at myself, and then unlocked the bathroom door and pulled it open. I'd left Jason in the kitchen of the open-concept house, but he was nowhere to be seen now. I pulled the bathroom door closed behind me, and he must have heard it, because suddenly he was calling out to me from somewhere in the house.

"I'm in the bedroom," he called, and I froze.

Straight there, huh? "Gimme a second, I'll be out!" Oh.

Okay.

Breathe, Reese.

He was probably doing a quick clean up, since I was an unexpected guest. What I could see of the rest of his home was incredibly tidy, which was surprising to me, for a man. My father had been a messy guy, and so had Gray. I was always on both of their asses about not being slobs, but I knew it was in vain. Those bad habits were ingrained.

Maybe it was a symptom of being a military man though. The kitchen opened into the living room, where a whole wall was dedicated to army paraphernalia. Framed flags and certificates, plaques, shadowboxes holding dog tags and medals. I took off my boots, leaving them beside his at the front door before I crept a little closer, tossing my purse on the couch as I went. My eyes widened over one particular medal.

"Hey Jason!"

"Everybody calls me Jay!"

"Sure Jason," I responded, grinning when I heard him let out a loud groan. "What's with the purple heart? Caught a piece of shrapnel to the head? Is that why you are the way you are?"

"Haha! Very funny!"

I giggled. "No, wait! I know! They gave you these to make up for experimenting on you, huh? You were a scrawny kid, and they pumped you full of stuff? Are you the failed test subject before Captain America?"

He full on laughed at that one, though it was muffled by distance. "Oh, I see you've got jokes, huh?"

I was still making my way down his wall of memories when I ran across the pictures, and the sight of him in his uniform honestly made my heart skip a beat. *So damned handsome*, I thought, then moved on to pictures of him and what I assumed to be friends, beside helicopters and other vehicles, pictures of them working. I was no military buff, but I knew a little. Unless I was mistaken, Jason was a sergeant, and in some of the pictures, it was almost like I could *see* the respect from lower-ranked soldiers as they watch him talk, or demonstrate something.

"Yeah, I've got *plenty* of jokes. Are you a supersoldier? What's your trigger word?"

"Well, I don't know about a trigger *word*," he said, from somewhere behind me. He was in the room with me, but I didn't turn around, pretending to be focused on the pictures. "But I damn sure believe you might be a trigger *person,* princess. Swear you make me crazy."

"What's wrong Sgt. Wright? Can't take a little challenge?"

I closed my eyes, sucking in a breath as Jason wrapped his arms around me from behind, pulling me tight against his chest. A whimper escaped my throat as he pressed his lips to my bare shoulder, trailing them up to my neck.

"You know," he said, his lips brushing my ear, "I like how "Sgt. Wright" sounds from you. It's about damned time you showed some respect and addressed me by my proper title."

Eyes still closed, I grinned. "Oh, well I'm definitely never saying that shit again."

"I bet you do," he said, sweeping my braids over my shoulder.

Reflexively, I tipped my head to the side, giving him better access to my neck, even as I opened my mouth to say, "I bet I don't."

Those words never came out.

Jason's mouth was delectably hot against my neck, sucking and biting and kissing until I involuntarily arched into him, feeling the heaviness of his dick pressed against the small of my back. I tried, in vain, to bite back a moan as he sucked hard enough to leave a mark, but when his tongue darted out to soothe the sting, I damn near melted against him.

He moved up to my earlobe, sucking the soft flesh into his mouth as his hands moved from my waist to underneath my dress. He groaned in my ear as his hands cupped my bare breasts and squeezed. They felt heavy in his hands, sensitive and hot as his thumbs danced over my nipples. Wetness pooled between my legs as they hardened into stiff peaks under his attention.

I arched against him again, purposely this time. He chuckled a little as he dropped one of his hands, gripping my thigh to urge my legs apart. I opened for him, moaning as his calloused hand cupped my sex, and squeezed.

"You're ready, huh?" he asked, dipping a thick finger into me. My only response was a sharp gasp as he did that again, pushing it deeper, the palm of his hand rasping over my clit as he pumped his finger into me. "I asked you a question, Reese." He pinched my nipple between his forefinger and thumb, gently tugging and teasing and making me thrust it further into his hand. He moved his hand from my breast, anchoring it around my waist to keep me still as he drove a second finger into me, plunging deep as he ground the heel of his hand against my clit. "*Reese…*"

"*Yes*," I moaned, breathless, as pressure began to mount deep in my core.

"Turn around."

"No. Do it like this," I mumbled. That was exactly what I wanted, from behind, with his hand on me while he slammed into me.

"*Turn. Around.*"

I shook my head, which apparently he didn't like very much.

He pulled his fingers from me and turned me around, and as soon as we were facing each other, I scowled.

"You asked about the purple heart," he said. There was the tiniest shred of anxiety in his voice, and that made me stop scowling, to actually listen. "This is why."

His moments in the bedroom must have been to change clothes, because now he was shirtless, with basketball shorts slung low on his hips. Jason's body was as gorgeous as he was – beautiful pecan skin spread over a thick, muscular frame, decorated with intricately detailed army tattoos. My eyes searched his arms and torso for a wound, for a scar, something to clue me in to what he meant.

And then my eyes dropped lower.

I could barely see them because of the length of his shorts, but Jason had powerfully built thighs. On his right side, his thigh led down to his knee, which led to an equally powerful calf. On the left, it led to his knee, which led to a prosthetic from the knee down.

My gaze shot back up to his, and I was surprised by the level of vulnerability I saw in his eyes. He swallowed hard, then cleared his throat. "Is this going to be a problem?"

What kind of question is that?

It caught me off guard for a couple of seconds, but my mind raced fast enough for a quick recovery. "Are you trying to be funny, *Jason*? Cause this isn't amusing."

His face dropped into a scowl. "*What*?"

"Don't *what* me. You brought me over here with the understanding that you'd be "hitting it right", and that's what I expect. Does your dick work?"

"Hell yeah my dick works!" he exclaimed, with an even deeper scowl.

"Then stop making excuses, *Sergeant*, and give me what I came over here for, damn."

I kept my gaze locked on his until understanding lit his eyes. His scowl softened, and he reached into his pocket, holding up the gold foil packet of a condom.

"Turn around. Put your hands on the wall. Spread your legs."

His voice was firm.

I did as he said, moving to an empty space on the wall. I tugged my dress up around my hips as he ripped the condom open, then pressed my palms to the wall. I shivered at the feeling of his hands on me again, caressing and squeezing my ass before he moved them to my waist. I sucked in a breath as his fingers slid over my stomach, up to my breasts again before his lips touched my shoulder.

He kept one hand cupped around my breast, then used the other to guide himself into me. We both let out a low groan of appreciation as he slid in, making me squirm as my body stretched for him. He filled me up, then didn't move, locking an arm around my waist to pull me close to him. His other hand moved from my breast to between my legs, pressing his thumb to my clit, just hard enough for me to feel it and want more. I tried to rock against his hand, but he held me still, squeezing me against him a little harder.

And *then* he began to move.

There was a burst of momentum as he plunged into me, hard, even though I would have sworn he was already buried as deep as he could go. That little move sent me up onto my toes with a sharp gasp of pleasure, followed quickly by another as he slid out of me just enough to do that again. I bit my lip hard, trying to hold my composure as he began to stroke. His moves were unhurried at first, carefully measured and delivered, stretching and teasing and pulling out stifled moans.

His thumb started moving against my clit – tight, slow circles, and I squeezed my eyes shut. He burrowed into me, not moving back, grounding his hips against mine, and it felt so good I damn near bit a hole through my lip.

He moved his hand from my waist, burying it in my hair to grip a handful of my braids. He tugged my head back, latching his mouth onto my neck and sucking hard, sending a deep shiver over my whole body. "Stop holding back," he growled in my ear, then gently bit me there, soothing the sting with a kiss after.

I whimpered something – hell, *I* don't even know what I was trying to say, but the next moment he started slamming into me with fast, deep, *powerful* strokes, and before I knew it, I was screaming. "*Jay, Jay, Jay*," over and over as he plunged into me. My whimpers, moans, cries of bliss were punctuated by the smack of skin on skin as the heady aroma of sex filled the air.

He lifted me by the hips, taking my feet off the ground as he drove harder. Weak with pleasure, there

wasn't much I could do except enjoy it. I braced my arms against the wall as pressure mounted in my core, rocking back, meeting him stroke for stroke, rolling my hips as much as I could. Somehow, he slid deeper again, his balls slapping against me as he moved. He used one arm around my waist to keep me up, then moved his other hand between my legs again.

As soon as he touched my clit, I came unglued.

"Ahhhhhh, Jay!"

A powerful shudder wracked my body as I came, sending tremors radiating all the way down to my toes. My throat was already raw, but I couldn't seem to stop crying out his name as wave after wave of pleasure rocked over me. I screamed again as he slammed into me one last time, with a thick growl in my ear as he released.

My breath was still coming in shallow pants, and tears streamed down my cheeks as Jason pressed his face to the back of my neck. I let out a heavy sigh as he lowered my feet back to the ground, then hurriedly tried to suck in more air. My heart was still racing when he tightened his arms around my waist, and planted several kisses along my shoulder. He was still inside of me, still throbbing, and my body reflexively clenched around him, again and again, like it was saying *more, more, more.*

"Goddamnit," he muttered, pushing his face against my neck again. "That was…"

"Incredible," I supplied, still out of breath. I swallowed hard, and then ran my tongue over my lips as I moved my hands from the wall, and placed them over his. My eyelids drifted closed as he pressed his lips to the little hollow behind my ear.

"I mean, I was gonna say it was *aiight*, but…"

He was out of me, and a few steps away in a flash, easily dodging my swatting hands. He chuckled as he jogged out, presumably toward the bathroom. I let my dress fall back to its proper place, though it was thoroughly wrinkled now, and stood there for a few awkward moments.

Okay… what now?

Contrary to my bold behavior, booty calls weren't really my thing… I hadn't thought to discuss with him how I was getting home. Was he driving me back to my car? Did I need to call a cab? Those thoughts were still running through my mind when I heard him come back into the room, and I turned around. He was standing there in the doorway to the hall, naked, and the sight made my breath hitch in my throat.

The shorts were gone now, so I could see all of him. Beautiful body, beautiful dick, even the complicated metal workings of his prosthetic were fascinating, and striking. New moisture built between my legs as my eyes raked over him.

Why does he have to be all sexy and friggin… bionic? Not fair.

Like he knew what I was thinking, a smirk spread over his face, and he held up the bath towel in his hands. He walked into the living room, spreading it over an armless chair, and then sat down.

Jason ran his tongue over his lips as he looked me over, then raised his arm, cocking a finger at me. "Get naked, and bring your ass here."

"And then what happened?" Devyn asked, her eyes wide as she leaned over the shelf at me. We were in Tones & Tomes, a local, black-owned bookstore that we both loved.

I lifted an eyebrow, then took a sip from my lowfat, low-sugar, low-fun latte. "What do you mean what happened?"

"I mean what did you do after he said that?!"

I sucked my teeth, wrinkling my face at my friend. "Girl what do you think I did? I got naked and took my ass over there! Did you forget I said that dick made me *cry*? Where the hell else would I go?"

Devyn erupted in giggles and I followed suit, laughing until my eyes watered. She grabbed me by the hand, pulling me down onto a bench in the quiet store, keeping her voice low.

"You know, I thought your ass had lost it when you texted me that you were going to that man's house.

But I'm starting to think it may have been your best decision this year. Like, have you seen yourself in a mirror? Forget *glowing*. Your ass is luminous."

I giggled again, blushing as I hung my head. It was Sunday afternoon, a time I almost always spent with Devyn, and my Friday night with Jason was still *very* fresh news.

We were up most of the night, sexing each other until we passed out. I woke up in his bed, feeling amazing, but sore. After a quiet, awkward good morning exchange, he drove me back into the city for my car, and

I hadn't seen or spoken to him in these two days since then.

Which was fine. I'd already gotten *exactly* what I needed, and beyond.

I pushed my braids out of my face, and shook my head. "Girl, I'm still trying to understand how the best dick of my life came from a man with a prosthetic leg. How the hell does any other man compete with that? He was picking me up, tossing me around like it was nothing, insane stamina, and his *body*… whew. It's really *not* fair."

Devyn laughed. "So when are you doing it again?"

I scoffed. "Girl, *bye*. I'm not."

"Are you crazy?!" Devyn asked, her voice rising as she took me by the shoulders. "Don't you dare do this to me!"

"To you?!"

She nodded. "Yes, to *me*. Girl, that story is the most action I've gotten in a *while* working these long ass shifts, and studying for the extra certifications for this job. I need you to fuck him again, for me."

"You are sooo stupid!" I laughed, shaking my head. "But nah, we don't even like each other, you know? I think the sexual chemistry was probably kinda destined to boil over eventually, but… no. It was much needed distraction for me that night, but that's all."

Devyn pouted, then playfully bumped my shoulder. "You're so mean. Won't even fuck that man again for your friend. Guess I gotta do it myself."

I started laughing again, but then Devyn's expression changed, shifting into more serious. "Wait, it's probably too soon for a joke like that."

I sucked my teeth. "Please –I know you wouldn't do any shit like that to me. Your name is *not* Olivia." Devyn got really quiet, looking at her hands, and picking imaginary dirt from her nails. I pushed out a little sigh, and rolled my eyes. "Go ahead and say it, I know you want to."

"Say what?" she asked, her eyes big with false innocence. "I don't even have nothing to say about that whole situation. Other than that I told you that bitch wasn't worth a damn. And neither was he. I mean, it's right in their names –

shady, grimy, shadowy gray ass Grayson, and sneaky, envious, snake green ass Olivia.

Even their parents knew they weren't gonna be shit, and named them accordingly."

That time, *my* eyes went wide, and I covered my mouth to keep from laughing. Devyn was crazy, but she

was right. I'd scrubbed my house free of any hints of Grayson, and I was glad I already had both feet out the door on that relationship before I found out about him and Olivia. That made it easy as hell not to spend any time crying because I was hurt– just pissed off at the betrayal, and glad to be done.

"Hey," she said, and I looked up. The anger was gone from her expression, but the seriousness remained as she met my gaze. "Outside of all of that though… how are you feeling?"

I let out a little sigh and then sat back, planting my hands beside me on the bench. "I feel okay. Like, *actually* okay."

We were two days past the anniversary of my father's death, and while I still wasn't feeling exactly myself, I was better than usual. The pain numbed a little more with each passing year, but it still hurt. This year, my recovery time was probably connected to the fact that I hadn't drunk myself into a stupor or drugged myself to sleep with prescription pills, which was how I'd spent the first years. I was trying to do better though. Natural methods to get to sleep when I had trouble, and distraction instead of self-medicating.

But whether or not a one-night stand was a

"healthier" coping method was pretty damned subjective. "Good," Devyn said, nodding as she patted my hand. "You know I laughed my ass off when E told me what you did at Refill, right?"

I shook my head. "I'm *so* not proud of that moment."

"Girl why? Cause *I* sure the hell am."

Devyn broke into another peal of laughter, and before long, I joined in. I was still laughing when I felt eyes on me, and glanced up.

My gaze fell right on Jason's.

I fought the urge to look away, and instead let my lips spread into a little smile. He was across the store, standing with an older man I recognized as the owner of the store, and another man who was a little shorter and slimmer than Jason, but sexy too.

Jason lifted his chin at me in a subtle acknowledgement, and then turned back to his conversation. I finally dropped my gaze, only to find Devyn looking at me with a huge grin.

"Is *that* Sgt. Wright?" she whispered, stealing a glance at the three men.

"In the olive shirt? Yeah."

Damn why did that color have to look so good on his skin?

He was in a deep green Henley that clung to his chest and stomach, with the sleeves pushed neatly up to his elbows. Dark jeans slung low on his hips, perfectly worn leather boots… I eased my braids over my chest, trying to hide my rising nipples.

"Girl…"

I looked back to Devyn. "What?"

She grinned. "That's it. That's the only word I can find."

"Trust me," I said, shaking my head. "I get it."

The group of men began to move, heading toward the back of the store. As they passed, I felt his eyes on me again, and looked up. He slowed down, watching me, and I cocked an eyebrow at him before me I rolled my eyes, wrinkling my nose at him. He shook his head, then shot me a wink as a sexy smirk spread over his lips.

My stomach clenched, and I squeezed my thighs together as I looked away. When he was gone, Devyn stood up, laughing as she reached for my hand to help me.

"Now," she teased, "After I just saw you react to him like that… Don't you dare tell me another lie about how you aren't sleeping with him again. I know a challenge when I see it."

nine

JASON

*F*ck Up Some Commas* blasted through my earbuds as I lifted the weight over my chest one last time. I took a breath, then racked the barbell, sitting up to nod my head at the gym employee spotting for me, before he moved on to another patron. I was done, and my muscles were exhausted.

Too bad it wasn't time to go home.

After my shower, it would be time to head to campus. I was *beyond* glad that once I finished this year, I'd be the proud owner of a shiny new mechanical engineering degree, with a focus on automotives. I wasn't gaining any new knowledge in the classes that actually related to my degree – just confirming what I'd already learned in the army. But, the internships I'd found in the field – at least the ones that led to the good jobs - wanted you to have the piece of paper, so the next thirty credit hours would find me at BSU.

I took my time cleaning off the weight bench, since nobody was waiting for it. Even though I had somewhere to be, I had to walk through the cardio area to get back to the showers, and I wasn't looking forward to that shit at all.

I made a mental note to get myself a weight set for home, sooner than later.

When I couldn't put it off anymore, I pulled out my phone, tugging the cord to my earbuds from its secure spot under my shirt. I hooked them up again, but nothing was playing. I just had the phone out, hoping that the sight of it would make these women leave me the fuck alone.

Apparently, I didn't have that kind of luck.

As I approached the area that housed the spin classes and didn't see the normal crowd outside, I got excited. *Hell yeah, they're already gone*, I thought.

Unfortunately for me, that wasn't the case. The door swung open as I approached, and about thirty women came streaming out. I didn't stop moving, but I saw them so they definitely saw me, and about two seconds later, it started.

"*Jaaay!*"

"*Awww!*"

"*I so admire your strength!*"

"*Do you need anything? Anything?*"

Plenty of men would have loved this type of attention, but I wasn't one of them. It was one thing for women to flock because they thought I was attractive – it was a whole other thing for me to get this attention out of pity.

The sympathetic looks made me sick to my stomach, and the sympathy pussy was even worse. I hadn't even really dated in the time I'd had my prosthetic, because every time a woman found out about it, she wanted to "help" me, and "take care" of me, instead of just treating me like a regular ass human being.

Obviously, that wasn't counting the ones who were freaked out by it, as it if I were contagious, or an invalid, or… shit, some type of alien controlling a life-sized human doll.

Fuck *all* of that.

I gave those women a weak smile, and kept walking, trying not to let it affect my mood. Logically, I

knew they didn't mean any harm. Just like when my dad and brothers worried too much, and got overbearing with the checking in and the phone calls. They did that because they cared. The women reacted like that to me because it was human nature to be sympathetic to a disability, it was what "decent" people did. On the basketball court, other men would act like I was delicate, or fragile, until I fouled somebody hard enough to make them mad. *Then* I could get a real game.

But I couldn't foul those spin class chicks into not feeling sorry for me, and nothing I said seemed to effect the treatment from my family. I just had to take it, and I'd be lying through my teeth if I said the shit didn't get tiresome, as well-meaning as they were.

Not the princess though.

I couldn't help the grin that spread over my face as I thought about Reese's reaction the other night. It was Tuesday now, four days since that unexpected run-in at

Sammy's had led to *other* unexpected things, and that image was still vivid as hell.

The way her expression changed when she realized what I was showing her – fascination, instead of pity. Her words – *does your dick work? Then stop making excuses and give me what I came for.* And her actions.

She hadn't been skittish about my ability to perform, or pick her up, or just handle her, physically. She was all into it, no hesitations. She trusted me to give her what she said she needed, without questioning my capability, and I was… honestly?

Grateful as hell for the experience.

I'd woken up way before she did the next morning, and went for a run to burn off residual sexual energy. It had been a minute for me, and I wanted to wake Reese up to go at it again, but once she woke up and was all extra quiet and shit, I figured it was for the best that I hadn't.

I didn't know if I'd fucked the mean out of her or what, but in the few times I'd seen her since then, she was different. Not in a bad way, just not the same. In the bookstore Sunday afternoon, in the library Monday… she hadn't been the woman I was slowly getting used to.

I wondered if I was going to see her today. I had a meeting with Professor B to discuss midterm grades, and the email to set those up had mentioned the possibility of her grad assistant sitting in on the meeting. We were given the chance to opt out and keep the meeting private, but of course, I hadn't. Because I wanted to see her, even if I couldn't explain why, not even to myself.

How did she feel about the other night?

Was she still upset about her little lame ass man doing her friend?

Was she still down about her father?

That stuff had been swirling in my mind since I dropped her off at her car Saturday morning, and still made rounds through my brain while I showered. If I saw her today… maybe I'd ask.

"Knock knock…"

The pen Reese was chewing on dropped from her hands as she looked up from her laptop. Her eyes searched the doorway for a second, then widened in recognition before she wiped her expression blank.

"Mr. Wright, the professor is running a little bit behind. There was an accident on the parkway, and she's stuck in that traffic. She'll be a few minutes. *Several* minutes. So if you want to reschedule, we can do that, or you can wait here, until she makes it in."

I blinked several times at the blandness of her response, and then studied her for a few moments. She had half her braids pulled into a ponytail right on top of her head, while the rest of them framed her face and rested on her shoulders. The oversized sweater she wore dipped low on one side, exposing the delicate gold chain around her neck, and one bare shoulder. It made me think about the dress she'd been wearing last Friday, which made me think about her being bent over in that dress last Friday.

"That's it? No smart remark? No insult, still?"

She shrugged. "I told you I wasn't engaging you while I was in official capacity here at the school. So yes, that's it."

"Oh, okay." I nodded. "I get that. I was thinking: Damn… maybe I really *did* fuck the mean out of her."

Reese's eyes went wide, and then she dropped her head, covering her face with her hand. I could tell she was trying her hardest not to laugh. Even when she looked up at me again with a scowl, those big browns of hers were sparkling with amusement.

"I'm not mean, I'm just not some little delicate flower. And even if I was… you didn't "fuck" anything out of me. I saw you and remembered you were sensitive, and went tattling to my mother last time. Are you waiting, or rescheduling?"

"I'll wait," I said, closing the door behind me, and chuckling as I sat down. "I'm done with classes for the day, so I'm not in any hurry. And for what it's worth, I had no idea she was your mother when I wrote that email."

"Sure you didn't."

"I *didn't*," I insisted. "How would I? It's not like y'all have the same last name, or look just alike."

She lifted an eyebrow. "You don't think we look alike?"

"Not enough that I noticed it with her in her glasses. I mean, I see it *now*, but before… nah."

She nodded. "Interesting. You're not very observant."

I laughed. "Here we go, huh?"

"What?" She smiled, leaning back in her chair as she played with the end of one of her braids. "That's not an insult, just an observation. Because I *observe.*"

"If you were so *observant*, you'd remember that I *did* fuck something out of you. *Jay, Jay, Jay, right there, Jay, oh my God, Jay,*" I said, imitating her feminine tone.

Once again, her eyes went wide, and she pressed her lips together tight to keep from smiling. "You sure you want to wait? Don't you need to, I don't know, go study, or go to work? Something. *Anything.*"

I shook my head. "Not today. Day off."

"And you want to spend it waiting to talk to your professor about your grade?"

"No," I grinned. "I want to spend it getting on your nerves."

She rolled her eyes. "You know, I really wish you wouldn't."

"What?" I scoffed. "Don't try to act like you don't enjoy this dynamic, like you aren't having fun."

Reese pulled her bottom lip into her mouth, scraping it between her teeth before she released it. That little action reminded me that with all the sexing we did that night, we hadn't kissed, and I couldn't think of a good reason why not.

"So… you're trying to "have fun" with me now?" she asked.

I shrugged. "Isn't that what we've been doing?"

"I guess you could say that. I'm just making sure you don't think something changed because we slept together."

I chuckled. "*Sleep* is the least of what we did."

"True." She eyed me for several moments, then let out a little sigh. "All of that *not* sleeping we did, and barely any foreplay. Are you always so eager?" Oh.

So *she* was thinking about what we hadn't done too.

"Me, the eager one?" I leaned forward over her desk, heard the little hitch in her breath, and smiled. "You were wet before I even touched you, princess. You're probably wet now."

She rolled her eyes. "So typically *male*, thinking that foreplay is just about getting you wet, instead of treating it like an important part of sex, to enjoy just as much as penetration."

"Oh I enjoy it plenty. Exploring, tasting, savoring, learning the sensitive areas on a woman's body. It's important to me."

She lifted an eyebrow. "But you didn't do that."

"Because that's not what you asked for. You asked to get fucked, so that's what we did. The other stuff is reserved for someone who belongs to me. You trying to belong to me?"

I was still leaning over the desk, my gaze locked with hers. When I said *that*, she broke the gaze, looking away and clearing her throat.

"*Belong*? Wow, Jason. I thought you were a lot more progressive than that. Thought you knew people only belonged to themselves. That they aren't objects for you to take ownership of."

I laughed. "I agree with that… generally speaking. But in a relationship, there's *absolutely* a certain justified sense of ownership. You're entering into an agreement – a partnership.

Your time, your body, your attention, your thoughts… your heart. That's not saying that you're that person's slave, or that they're yours.

That's not saying somebody has to bow to your ideals, or follow your commands. But because of the desired, reciprocal connection, yes… a part of them belongs to you, while you're together.

That's why we get pissed about cheating, right?

Especially "emotional" affairs. They betrayed you, gave away something you thought was yours. Gave away your laughs, your orgasms, your moans, your quiet contemplations. The shit *you* wouldn't dare give somebody else. It may not be "progressive" or politically correct, but hey… I never claimed to be either. I'm just speaking my mind."

She nodded. "Okay. I guess I see your point. But you can't be throwing around the word "belong" all willy-nilly around here. The professor would've lit your ass up."

I chuckled. "And I would've accepted my asslighting and still argued my point. Wouldn't budge." "You think you could handle her?"

"I handle *you* don't I?

Reese shook her head, showing me that pretty smile she seemed to like keeping closely guarded when

I was around. "I let you *think* you're handling me."

"Nah, I let *you* think you're not getting handled."

The smile stayed. "What's your story, Jason Wright?"

"My story?"

She nodded. "Yeah. Military vet, mechanic– slash–car salesman, student, asshole… amputee. How did life bring you *here*?"

"Oh, so you're interested in me now, huh?" I grinned.

"You know what… yes. I am."

I shrugged. "Okay. I'm the youngest of three boys—"

"Which is why you're a crybaby. Makes sense."

I laughed. "Are you gonna let me tell it?"

"Yes, continue please."

"Like I said, youngest of three boys. We're 28, 31, and 34. By the time I was graduating high school, the college money had been exhausted between my brothers, and I didn't want to add more financial burden to my parents. And, I wasn't interested in school anyway."

"Really?" Reese asked, sounding genuinely shocked. "But you're obviously sma—I mean, you don't seem completely stupid. Why wouldn't you want to go to school?"

"Did you almost give me a compliment just then?!"

She laughed, then pretended to wipe sweat from her brow. "*Almost did.* That was a close one, wasn't it?"

"It really was," I chuckled. "But yeah, as far as school, I just didn't really know what I wanted to do.

Seemed like a waste of time. If I'd stayed home, Dad would have put me to work at the dealership—"

"The dealership?"

"Yeah, J&P. My father is the owner."

Her eyes nearly bugged out of her head before she quickly schooled her features into a neutral expression.

"Interesting."

"Interesting?" I asked, narrowing my eyes. "How so?"

"No reason."

"Reese…"

"It's nothing, really. Just… your father is a really nice, handsome, charming guy. *Nothing* like you, at all. I never would have thought you were related. Not even a little. At all."

"Daaaamn," I laughed. "For your information, I take after my mother. Do you wanna hear the story or not?"

"Sorry. Continue."

"Thank you. I didn't want to work at the dealership, so army it was. I learned a lot, saw a lot, saved up some money, sent some home to help my family. No regrets."

"So you enjoyed it?"

I scoffed. "I *loved* it. Traveled places I never would have imagined, doing something I loved – working with machines. I can build, or fix, an engine for anything. Mechanics are *vital* in the military, especially in a war zone, limited resources. Definitely got my fill of danger."

Reese's eyes went wide. "I bet. So why'd you leave? Because of your leg?"

Her voice softened over that question. I didn't get the impression that she felt bad for asking, but that she thought it may be a touchy subject for me. And in a way, it was, but *her* approach wasn't bothersome at all to me.

"Yeah," I nodded, relaxing back into my chair. "I had my dream assignment – helicopter repair. Bad-ass

Apaches. So, I'm over there, me and my team have to do a retrieval of a broken bird, because if it's still possibly functional, we can't just leave it there to get used against us. We find it. Fix it. Get it up in the air to fly back, and

suddenly we're not alone anymore. Um… long story short, there was enemy fire, and then there was a crash. I'm blessed that half of a leg is all I lost. Everybody on the assignment wasn't as lucky."

"That's *terrifying*," she said quietly, shaking her head. "You still think about it a lot? Nightmares? Trouble sleeping?"

"What, like from the crash, and the combat?" – she nodded – "Nah, not really. I guess I got lucky with that too, because I don't have nightmares, I'm not scared of loud noises… no triggers, nothing like that. I know that's not the case for everybody that goes through something traumatic, but I'm just happy to be alive."

Again, she nodded. "I get that. And, you found something you like, that can turn into a career. I saw that you're pursuing mechanical engineering. And almost done."

"So you've been scoping me out, huh?"

She wrinkled her nose. "*No*…yes." She laughed.

"I'm a big girl, I can admit my curiosity. Wondering how you can write so eloquently, and have these views that aren't steeped in patriarchy, and yet be… *you.*"

We both laughed at that, and I shook my head.

"Like I said earlier, I'm just speaking my mind. I'm supposed to give an opinion, so I did. But growing up, my mother wasn't having all of that "a woman's place" this, and "get you a white girl" that. Not to say that my father *was* on that, but my mother was the one who drilled it in us. The value of our blackness, the value of a black woman as a person, and a partner, not how much sex she does or doesn't have, or if she can cook, all of that. Just stuff that oughta be common sense. And we *stayed* at Tones & Tomes. Every Saturday morning."

"It was Sunday afternoons for me," Reese said, smiling. "Me, my mother, my best friend, and her mother.

Our weekly "girl's day"."

"See there? My worldview sparked from the same place yours did. A mama who didn't take any shit."

She nodded. "Indeed."

There was silence for a few moments before I leaned forward again, and asked, "What about you?"

Reese lifted an eyebrow. "What *about* me?"

"What's your story? I gave you my condensed autobiography, I want to hear yours too."

She cringed. "Oh. Um... I don't really have one."

"Bullshit. Stop stalling."

Shaking her head, she laughed, then leaned forward over the desk too, propping her elbows on the dark surface and resting her chin on her hands. "Um... Only child. Parents divorced when I was fourteen. My father was a jazz musician. "The Reggie Alston Band." A big dreamer, and a creative, and he instilled that in me.

Academics came from mama. But anyway... um, when I was twenty years old, he died. And it broke my heart, because I loved my daddy, I still *needed* my daddy."

She wasn't looking at me anymore – she was looking down at the desk instead, unblinking, until finally she cleared her throat. "Uh… I completely broke down. I got kicked out of school because my grades tanked, and I was drinking, and fighting, hanging with some not-sogreat people and… just not in a good place. I wasn't very happy with myself, but I realized that I was hurting the people who were still here who loved me. And I realized I was fucking up my dream, and knew my father would be devastated if he could see that. So, I cleaned myself up, did what I needed to get re-enrolled in school, and

I'm working on keeping the promise that I made to him, that I would fulfill my dream."

I smiled at her when she looked up, pretending I didn't notice the gloss in her eyes. "What's the dream?"

"Well," she said, perking up. "If this MFA program doesn't destroy my soul first, eventually I want to teach a Creative Writing course, here at BSU. With a lot of writing courses, there's so much focus on "proper technique" and "rules" and all of that. I want to teach people how to – productively – write from the heart."

"How do you *teach* somebody to write from the *heart*?"

She smiled. "Instilling confidence, and encouraging individuality. Stripping away fear, burying the need to compete. Feeding *real* creativity, critiquing based on an understanding of an individual's voice, instead of a guidebook on what's right and wrong. Of course, there *are* certain rules, like grammar and spelling that should serve as the roadmap, but there's a way to combine the two without losing the soul of the writing. A lot of times, we learn to write a certain way, and don't figure it out until vital years have gone by. So as *I'm* learning, I'm figuring out how I can teach it to others. It's still just a concept now, and not the "coolest" thing in the world I guess, but… that's what I want to do."

"I think it's cool as hell."

She lifted her head, surprised. "Really?"

"Yeah. I mean, maybe some of the people who end up taking your class will be writers who *could* have been Corey Jefferson. Sounds like you'll be providing an important public service to me."

Reese laughed, sweeping a handful of braids behind her back as she sat up. "You know, maybe thinking about that will make some of these classes a little easier on me."

"You're welcome."

"Thank you." She held my gaze for a long moment, and then pulled her lip between her teeth.

"Hey… do you—"

"I am *so* sorry Mr. Wright," Professor Bryant said as she breezed into the office, interrupting whatever Reese had been about to say. She blew out a big sigh as she headed to her desk, and then looked at me with a smile as she motioned for me to come over. Reese had already turned her eyes back to her laptop, and kept them there while I moved to Professor B's desk. When she was ready to start, she called Reese over.

The professor reached down to dig something out of her bag, and I caught Reese's eye again, giving her a wink. Just like in the bookstore the other day, she blushed, and that made me happy as hell for some reason.

Huh.

Maybe I *was* into bougie girls.

ten.

"What's on your mind, little girl?"

My mother's eyes met mine through her mirror as she slid the back on a pair of diamond studs. I grinned at her, then shrugged.

I was in her bedroom, on her side of our duplex,

watching her get ready to go out. It wasn't exactly a ritual, but ever since I was a teenager, once she was serious about someone, she'd let me – and usually Devyn – sit in her room while she dolled up, laughing through questions she mostly didn't answer. In the twelve years since my parents divorced, I'd seen my mother get ready for a healthy amount of dates, even if I never saw the

guy. She had this thing about bringing men around me – wouldn't do so until they'd been dating three or four months. That remained true even through adulthood – I hadn't seen Joseph since that day at the dealership.

"Thinking about you and your new boo. Y'all have been at it for how long?"

She smiled, then picked up a tube of deep red lipstick. "Two months now. It flew by." *Yeah,* I thought. *It has.*

Because if it had been two months for them, that meant it had already been two months since that first office meeting with Jason. A month and a half since that car drop off that had lit my little panties on fire for him.

A month since that night at his house.

A whole sexless month.

I almost wished we hadn't done it, because something had shifted. When I thought about him now, instead of sexual curiosity tainting my disdain for him, it was a just plain old curiosity, no ill feelings. What was he

doing, what was he thinking about… who was he with? Was he wondering the same things about me? Within the span of two months, I'd gone from patent distaste to liking – as in *wanting* – him, and I really didn't know how to feel about that.

I wasn't ready to like anybody right now.

My midterms had gone well, despite my emotional state, and I was chugging along. I had been able to keep up with my own course work, plus the things I had to do for my assistantship, with little to no major problems.

Things were just now starting to feel somewhat normal again, after the bullshit with Olivia and Gray. He wasn't calling anymore, I was over ducking and dodging her in the halls, and I really just didn't have the extra energy to expend on anger for either of them. They could have each other.

Overall, life was good for me. I'd fallen into a groove, found just the right balance. When I was busy, or with my mother, or Devyn – basically with my family – I was really happy, and at peace, which I hadn't been able to say in a while. It was the other times that were getting to be a little tricky.

I could enjoy my own company. Loved my own company, which was important to me because of the way things went after I lost my father. I could read, surf the internet, watch TV – I still wasn't allowed back at Refill – do any number of things alone, and be perfectly okay with that… most of the time. But like almost any other human being, sometimes I craved human interaction.

Male human interaction.

A male human named Jason.

"Did you know your silver fox was Jason Wright's father?" I asked my mother, keeping my voice casual, and light. She hadn't said anything about it yet – didn't really volunteer information about her boo at all – but I'd been trying to think of a way to broach the subject without seeming nosy.

She lifted an eyebrow at me, then focused on the mirror to swipe mascara across her lashes. "Not when we first met, but eventually, yes. I knew before we went to the dealership."

"Wait, what?" I wrinkled my nose. "I thought the dealership *was* when you first met?"

My mother put the tube of mascara back into place on her vanity, and then turned to face me.

"Technically it was, but not exactly."

"Okay…? What does that even mean, mama?"

She let out a little sigh, and a smile crossed her face that seemed almost… *embarrassed.* "We kind of

"met" online."

"What?!" I snatched myself from my reclined position on her bed, sitting up on my knees. "Online?! Like online dating? Like… *fifty-shades-of-gray-hair-dotcom*?!"

"You're *not* funny, little girl," she scolded, finger pointed, even though I could tell she was fighting a smile.

"And no, not a dating site. There was an online community for jazz lovers in the area, jamsession.com. It shut down about a year ago, but some of the members made a chat group thing for the members who wanted to keep in touch."

I scooted to the end of the bed, super interested in what she was saying, and super excited that she was actually saying it. "Okaaay… *and*?"

"And…," she sighed. "Well, neither of us had a profile image, because that was part of the appeal. We were people from all over, talking about artists, music, connecting over that shared interest. But sometimes me and "Jazzy Joe" would end up in a separate conversation about other things."

I grinned. "So he… what, inboxed you or something?"

"What?"

"Like a private chat?"

She nodded. "Yes, a private chat. And as we talked, we got closer, little things would get shared. Life, and relationships, and personal philosophies… and more little tidbits. One of those was that he owned a car dealership. That didn't really stand out to me until I needed a car, and I remembered his mentions of J&P."

My eyes went wide. "So you didn't tell him you were coming?!"

She shook her head. "Absolutely not. We hadn't made a plan to meet up or anything, even though we'd hinted at it. I figured I could go, get a look at him.

Satisfy a bit of curiosity."

I laughed. "Mmm*hmmm*! You weren't expecting

all that salt and pepper fineness to run up on you like that, were you?!"

Her mouth spread into a wide grin, and she laughed too. "No… no, I certainly wasn't."

"This is hilarious," I giggled. "And friggin' adorable. I mean, I wondered why my cool, collected mama was all giggly over this man she just met, and now

I see! You were already crushing on him!"

My mother shrugged, then bent to rub a shimmering body cream onto her legs. "Maybe a little."

"Oh please," I teased. "Does he know who you are?"

"I told him that night when he called. He thought it was sexy."

"He called it sexy because *you're* sexy," I laughed. "Otherwise he would have called the police.

What's your username?"

Her head popped up, eyes wide. “Oh Reesie. I’ve already said too much. I’m not telling you that.”

JASON

“Who is “boogie_woogie_woman” and what you showing her tonight that she’s not gonna forget? Y’all being nasty ain’t you?”

I hopped out of the way just in time to avoid getting swung on by my dad.

I was already at his house, which he knew, and had come up the stairs looking for him. I found him in his office, with his back to the door, so immersed in whatever was happening on his laptop that he didn’t even hear me come in. Curiosity drew me closer, and I peeked over his shoulder to read what was on the screen.

“I oughta knock your head in,” Pops warned, rising from his seat. He closed the lid of the computer, glaring at me.

I lifted my hands in a soothing gesture. “My bad, Pops,” I chuckled. “I wasn’t trying to be in your business like that, I swear. I thought you were looking at new cars for the lot or something, not… *that*. Does your lady friend know you're chatting with "boogie woogie women" online?"

"My lady friend *is* boogie_woogie_woman, and your ass needs to learn how to knock. What you want, boy?"

"I was just coming to tell you I finished getting up those leaves in the front yard for you."

His glare softened into a concerned frown, and he propped his hands at his waist. "What are you doing messing around with yard work? I told you I'd hire somebody."

"For what? You've got three grown ass sons who live in the same city."

"Yeah, but Joseph is always at the hospital, Justin is always on a deadline, and you're..."

I crossed my arms. "I'm what? Able, available, and willing to rake the yard? *That's* what you were going to say, right?"

He let out a heavy sigh. "Point taken. I just... I worry about you, son. I don't want you out there straining yourself with that."

I swallowed the redundant argument that I was easily the strongest, most physically fit of my brothers, even with an "impairment" and that I'd done a more thorough, quicker job than anybody he probably would hired. Instead, I forced a smile to my face, hoping it didn't look like a grimace. "Well, in any case, it's done." Pops drew his head back, looking at me in surprise. "What, no argument there? No insistence that you can handle it, that you're not a little boy anymore.

No rejection of my fatherly concern?"

I shrugged, then dropped into the empty chair behind me. "Nah."

For several moments, my father studied at me, not saying anything, before a smile spread over his face.

"What's her name?"

I lifted an eyebrow. "Who?"

His smile grew wider, and he shook his head, chuckling. "Your sandpaper."

At first, I just stared at him, confused, until the memory of my mother's words made me laugh. "What makes you think I found some?"

"You've been mighty laid back these last few weeks. I didn't have to ask you to change out of the service center uniform before you came out on the floor yesterday. You haven't been walking around here like you were insulted by folks caring about you."

"So that means I found a woman?"

He nodded. "And she must be a doozy too, to soften you up. Coarse grit."

I tried to keep a smile off my face. Reese wasn't my girl, but she was the only person even close, and

"coarse grit" was accurate. She was nobody's shrinking violet, not afraid to speak her mind, eager to do verbal battle. Hell, maybe physical too. On the other side of that, she was funny as hell to me, compassionate without being patronizing, and passionate about the things she believed in. Not to mention she was smart, and so damned sexy it didn't make sense. She was very, *very* Reese. Unapologetically.

And I liked that. A *lot.*

"You're grinning pretty hard, son," Pops said, chuckling as he left the room. "Start deciding how much you want to spend on the ring."

"Wait, *what*?" I jumped up, following him into his bedroom as he sat down, slipping a pair of leather brogues on his feet. I noticed then that he was dressed like he was headed out, in slacks and a button up shirt.

He stood up, lifting a tie from his dresser, and looping it around his neck. "I said start deciding how

much—"

"Nah, I heard you," I said, holding up a hand. "I'm just saying... nah, it's not like that. Nowhere near like that. We aren't even dating."

"What's stopping you?"

"I... don't really know. She did just break up with somebody like a month ago."

My father stopped fixing his tie, looking at me with a raised eyebrow. "What the hell that have to do with you?"

I shrugged. "Aren't you supposed to give somebody time after that?"

He laughed. "Boy, if she's got you grinning like that, she's had plenty of time. Trust your old man. I knew my way around women until I met your mother. I forgot all of my "swag" as you young fellas call it," he said, still chuckling. "That's probably what's wrong with you now. Woman got your head messed up."

"My head isn't messed up though."

"Mmmhmm. Talk to me about it again in six months." He sprayed himself with cologne, and then pulled a sweater over his head. "Now if you'll excuse me, I'm heading to go pick up my woman, because *I* know how to ask a pretty girl out."

- & -

"If he thought your little super sleuthing was sexy, wait until he sees *this*. Damn, mama!"

"Language, Reesie."

"Sorry."

Still. *Daaaamn, mama!*

She was going to give that man a heart attack in that dress. It was a little black sweater knit number, with an asymmetric hem that rode high on her thighs. Her legs were covered, protected against the cold by opaque black tights, but the lack of skin didn't diminish the effect. Up top, she was covered all the way to her neck, but the material of the dress hugged and accentuated her fit curves.

She chuckled as she slid her feet into tall boots.

"You young girls aren't the only ones who can keep a man's attention."

"Gone with your bad self then," I laughed. "He's coming to pick you up?"

Mama nodded. "Yes, which means you need to scoot your little booty right on over to your own house please."

"I can't stay to see you off on your date?"

"You mean be nosy?"

"That's exactly what I mean."

She shook her head as she checked her appearance in the full-length mirror, adjusting a few hairs, smoothing over her dress. "Then absolutely not.

Get yourself some business little girl. Shouldn't you be… I don't know, out with Devyn?"

"Devyn is studying, and then she has a certification exam tomorrow."

"Other friends?"

I frowned. "I'm not feeling super trusting toward anybody except Devyn after that mess with Olivia. I'm still cooling off."

"*Definitely* get that." She turned around, studying me for a few moments. "What about you and Mr.

Wright? What's going on there? Don't think I haven't noticed the googly eyes."

"Googly eyes?! What googly eyes? There were no googly eyes!"

"Whatever you say, sweetheart." Her mouth spread into a knowing smile. "But you could do much, *much* worse than a young man like Jason Wright. He's intelligent, grounded, he's seen the world, and he's not a stuffy, stuck up, intellectual type, like what you usually go for even though they do nothing for you."

I lifted an eyebrow. "Okay, first… you don't think it's weird to push me to date your boyfriend's son? Second, I *have* done worse, remember? Third… what do you mean they do nothing for me? I would think you'd want me to go for a suit and tie kind of man."

"Why? I'm not into those types, why would I want that for you?"

I shrugged. "Culture, stability—"

"Ennui…," she said, rolling her eyes. "Trust me – you want a man that lights a fire in you. Your father did that for me. Now, our relationship didn't work because he couldn't keep his penis just between us, but one thing I can't say is that I have any regrets about the time he was mine. I know you, my dear. And I've not gotten to see it first hand, but based on what I *have* seen, I know Mr.

Wright stokes your little heart flames."

I didn't bother denying it. I just looked away.

"To address your other concerns, there's no blood relation dear, first of all. And," she said, stepping over to where I was still kneeling on the bed. She raised a hand to my face, lifting my chin to look me in the eyes. "Of course I remember that you haven't always made the best choices in partners. But I certainly wish *you* would forget. It was the past, Reesie. You made a mistake, and you did what you were supposed to do when you realized it. Nothing that happened after that is your fault. Do *you* remember that?"

I pulled my lip between my teeth, and nodded.

"Yes, mama."

"Good." She smiled. "I know I've spent enough time over the last six years trying to get it through your big head."

"My head isn't big!"

She twisted her mouth. "I pushed you out, child.

My vagina would beg to differ."

"Mama *ewwww*!" I squealed, laughing as she pulled me into a hug.

"I love you Reesie."

"I love you too."

"Okay," she said, swatting my butt. "Now get on, get out of here. I was serious about you not being here when Joseph arrives. Who knows if we'll actually make it out of the house?"

"*Mama!*"

This is crazy.

I thought those words at least a billion times between going back to my house, logging on to my BSU dashboard, and hunting down the contact information all of my mother's students had given her at the beginning of the semester.

Were the ethics a little questionable? Perhaps.

But if we were thinking it through, I'd already slept with one of my mother's students, and she was dating his father. Me looking up his cell number had to be lower on the list of violations than *any* of that.

Once I had it in front of me, I punched it into my phone, and then promptly deposited my phone on the coffee table in front of me.

This is crazy.

There was no way I was about to call this man, unannounced, using a phone number he hadn't given to me. At least that's what I told myself, all the way up until the point that the phone was against my ear, and I was listening to the tone as it rang.

Once.

Twice.

A third time.

Okay, so he wasn't answering.

Should I let it go to voicemail?

Should I leave a message?

Should I hang up now?

Yeah, you should hang up now.

Now!

"Hello?"

I dropped the phone to my lap in surprise, and then hurriedly snatched it back up, pressing it to my ear.

"Hello?" I asked, hoping he hadn't hung before I could right my awkwardness.

"Hello…?"

Dear God, what kind of sorcery was it that he could possibly sound *better* over the phone? Or… shit, what if it wasn't him?

"Um, I was calling to speak to Jason."

Silence, and then a quiet chuckle. "Reese, it's me. This is Jay."

"Oh! Okay. How did you know it was me?"

"Well," he said, taking a deep breath. "Nobody's voice has quite the same mean-sexy-bougie blend as yours. It's distinctive."

I bit the inside of my cheek, trying not to smile even though I was alone. "Ha ha. Funny."

"Wasn't trying to be funny, I was being honest.

How'd you get this number?" – *Oh, shit! I didn't even think about how I was going to explain that* – "I'm going to assume an abuse of power, but I'll let it slide this time if you answer a question for me," he said. His voice was suddenly muffled, like he was moving around, and balancing the phone against his ear. "Settle a debate between me and this girl – you're cooking spaghetti, right? Break the noodles or leave them whole?" Girl?

What girl?

Who the fuck was he cooking with at nine o'clock on a Friday night?

I mumbled something about how "*everybody knows you're supposed to break them in half, stupid*," and then something unintelligible about having to go. I ended the call, and sat there wondering what kind of non-

cooking ass girl he had at his place that didn't know you were supposed to snap the goddamn noodles before you put them in the damn pot, even if the box didn't say that.

Ugh!

I completely understood how irrational it was to be fuming about this, for several reasons: I didn't know who he had over. It wasn't my business anyway. I didn't know why she was over there. It wasn't my business anyway. It had been a month since we slept together. It wasn't my business anyway. Even if it had been *a day* since we slept together, we didn't have any type of commitment. He didn't owe me anything. *And it wasn't my business anyway.*

But I *wanted* it to be my business.

I fell over onto my side, burying my face in the soft pillows that decorated the couch. My problem of wanting to talk to, wanting to *see* Jason wouldn't actually be a problem if I'd worked up the courage to just do it before now. I'd started to, the day we were together in the office, ask him if he wanted to grab a late lunch after. It was bold for me, and I surprised my damned self when I opened my mouth to actually say the words.

It had the power of spontaneity behind it. I wasn't thinking about anything except how much, in that moment, I was enjoying talking with him. At this point,

Jason knew things about me that Gray didn't even know, had never cared to ask, and it felt good to be in the moment like that with somebody other than Devyn or my mother. Having shallow fun and good sex was one thing – a real connection was something totally different.

And then it was interrupted.

Maybe it had been a one time thing… right? It was crazy to think that we could replicate what I felt in that moment when he said my dream was valuable. Or when he referenced a romance novel to me, or teased me about the sounds I made during sex, or— Shit.

My phone started ringing, and it was him.

I slid it away from me.

Instead of sitting there and staring at it, I got up and did something – *anything* – else. I took a shower, played in my braids, painted my toenails, rearranged my Tupperware and cleaned out my refrigerator. By the time I stopped forcing myself to not look at my phone, almost two hours had passed.

The little blue LED on top was blinking, taunting me, reminding me that there was a missed call, and I was going to have to address it, at some point.

I picked up the phone like it was hot, and slid my fingers across the screen to unlock it. Turns out there was not only a missed call, but a text message too.

"Hey, I think we got disconnected. You were saying something, but it was muffled, and then the call dropped. Hit me back. – Jason."

Yes, I'd already saved the number in my phone.

For a few minutes, I sat there, biding my time, not wanting to seem too eager with a quick text back. But then I realized he'd sent it almost two hours ago. *Shit.*

I had to respond now.

"Yeah, bad signal or something. I didn't want anything though. Didn't mean to interrupt anything with your girl."

So that was slightly petty, and I knew that when I hit send. What was *more* petty, and unintentionally so, was sending that kind of message at this time of night, when they were probably still together. I wasn't *that* kind of girl.

"My girl? Are you talking about Brielle? – Jason." I frowned.

"Uhh, I guess so? The one who didn't know how to cook spaghetti?"

"Ha! Well, she's only six years old, and the box doesn't say to break the noodles. Don't judge her too hard. ;) – Jason." Oh.

So…

"And she's my niece. – Jason." *Whew.*

"Yeah, I thought it was probably a little kid."

"You realize that contradicts your statement just a couple of texts ago? You ain't gotta lie, princess. – Jason."

"And you had to want something, or you wouldn't have called. So, what's up? – Jason."

"Nothing really. You still babysitting?"

I flinched when my phone went off, notifying me that instead of just texting back, Jason had decided to call. I took a deep breath, then slid my thumb across the screen, allowing the call to connect.

"You know this is a pet peeve for some people, right? Responding to a text with a phone call? You don't have any kind of manners."

Jason chuckled, and I had to clench my thighs in response to the warmth of that sound. "I don't give a damn about that. I don't feel like typing."

"Well, I don't feel like *talking*."

"But you sound so damned good, with your little late night sexy phone voice."

"What?" I laughed. "I don't have a 'late night sexy phone voice', fool."

"The hell you don't. Over there sounding like Girl Six."

"Oh *wow*. A phone sex operator, huh? Is that where your paycheck goes, why you were acting funny about paying for dinner the other night?"

"Exactly. Glad you understand," he chuckled.

"Mmhmm. You didn't answer my question."

"What question was that?"

"If you were still babysitting or not…"

"Nah. I was at my dad's house when you called earlier, watching her for my brother. I actually just walked in the door about twenty minutes ago myself."

I sat back on the couch, snuggling deep into the pillows. "And what are you doing now?"

"Talking to you. Duh. Waiting on you to stop playing and go ahead and swing through."

"Why do *I* have to swing through?" I asked. "Don't tell me *just* when I was starting to think better of you, you're gonna prove yourself to be the bum ass dude I thought you were?"

He chuckled. "Damn, I gotta be a *bum* though?"

"Mmhmm." I rolled over onto my side. "Why should I have to go out in the cold? If you wanna see me, you can come to me."

"Oh, it's like that?"

"Yeah, it's like that."

There were a few seconds of silence, and then he said, "Aiight. I'll be there in thirty minutes." *Wait, what?!*

"Have you eaten yet? It's kinda late, you probably already had dinner, huh?"

Oh shit, he's serious!

I jumped up from my spot on the couch, nearly tripping over the ottoman as I looked around, making sure my house was clean enough for company. "Umm… no, actually." I really hadn't, but I was hoping he'd offer to stop and grab something, which would give me a little more time to prepare.

"Cool," he said, already sounding like he'd gotten up and started moving. "I'll bring you some of me and Bri's spaghetti. I mean, it's the least I can do since you did help."

"Uh, yeah. That would be cool."

Silence again. And then, "Just so we're on the same page… I'm not like, expecting anything from you, once I'm there."

"I didn't think you were, but… I appreciate you wanting to be clear."

"Yeah. Aiight so… thirty minutes?"

I looked around at my already spotless apartment, then my clean, well-moisturized skin and neatly painted toenails from my little binge earlier, when I was trying to avoid my phone.

"Yeah. Thirty minutes."

eleven.

JASON

"I should make your ass wait outside."

I grinned at Reese as she stood in her doorway, arms crossed, looking comfortable and collegiate in an oversized blue Blakewood State University hoodie. Little by little, she was blowing my initial perception of her out of the way. I would have bet money that knowing I was coming by, she would have gotten dressed up, intending to tease. Instead, she stood in front of me in a hoodie, shorts, and fuzzy socks, no makeup, with her braids loose, hanging around her shoulders and face.

"Why would you want to do that?" I asked, straightening to full height. Reese was maybe 5'6-7" to my 6'4", and that difference of almost a foot made her have to tilt back a little to look me in the face.

"Because you said *thirty* minutes, and according to my phone, it's only been twenty-two. What if I wasn't ready yet?"

"Just barely got off the toilet before I rang the bell, huh?"

She wrinkled her nose, and laughed. "*Eww!* No! Come in, it's cold."

She took the large Tupperware container from me as she stepped back to allow me inside. Her home was warm – in temperature and feel – decorated in purples, earthy grays, and eclectic wooden accents. I wasn't surprised, even a little, that her walls were lined with the work of black artists. I grinned at the glass case of vinyl records, with a vintage player. A few of the covers were on display, all featuring the same group – her father's.

"Shoes off please," she said, closing the door behind me. She walked off toward the kitchen without looking back, and I called after her.

"I can't get any help?"

She stopped walking and turned to me, face twisted. "For *what*? Don't your fingers work?" She went back to what she was doing, and I tried not to smile as I bent to remove my shoes, and left them by the door.

When I went into the kitchen, she was pushing herself onto her toes to slide the bowl of spaghetti into the microwave over the stove. The little white yoga shorts she was wearing rose up with her, almost giving a peak of what was underneath. The bottom hem reached that sexy little cuff of her ass and stopped, then lowered again as she started the microwave and turned around.

"Hey," she said, "You didn't really need help in there did you?"

I chuckled. "Nah."

She pushed out a little sigh. "Okay. Good. I was hoping you were kidding. I don't want you to think I *won't* help, if you need it, but—"

"You're good," I said, raising my hand in front of me. "I was just playing around."

She nodded. "Okay. Cause it didn't seem like you needed any, so I honestly thought it would be kind of offensive if I offered. *Damn*!" She snapped her fingers.

"Missed opportunity. Next time I'll be on top of it."

"You really are something else." I stepped further into the kitchen, moving closer to where she was.

She smiled. "I am, aren't I? A special breed."

"More like a special *case*. A *nut* case."

"Oh whatever," she said, her eyes dancing with laughter before she turned away, going to her refrigerator.

"I made us a little salad, and um… if you're staying long enough to sober up after, I opened a bottle of wine."

I chuckled. "Oh, shit! You're turning this into a whole romantic dinner thing, huh?" Her eyes went wide, lips parted, and then she looked away, dropping her eyes to the salad bowl in her hands. "Nah, don't get embarrassed now," I said, laughing as I took the bowl from her, and sat it down on the counter. "I mean, I'm down with it, I just wasn't expecting it."

I put my hand to her waist, and she immediately responded, stepping closer and relaxing against me like it was second nature. Her braids grazed my hand as she tipped her head up. "I got nervous, I guess. Started doing too much. If you hadn't gotten here early, I probably would've had that fireplace lit."

I threw my head back and laughed. "Wow. I can't imagine you nervous. You seem very, *very* sure of yourself."

"Well, I guess my secret is out now. I'm not as impossibly perfect as I look." Those words were barely out of her mouth before she broke into a peal of giggles.

"You couldn't even say that shit with a straight face, huh?"

Wearing a big smile, she shook her head. "I couldn't. But yeah, I get nervous just like anybody else when I…"

"When you…?" She dropped her gaze again, pulling her lip between her teeth. I brought my free hand up to her face, tipping her chin up. "When you what, princess?"

Her eyelids fluttered closed for a second, and then she turned those big browns on me. "When I… like somebody."

"Oh, so you *like me* now, wow! I thought you didn't like "grimy, egotistical, stupid mechanics who can't stay on the subject of the paper"? What happened to that, huh?" I dropped my hands to her ass, squeezing as I pulled her in closer. "Dick changed your mind, didn't it?"

"Here you go with that exaggerating again," she laughed. "I didn't say all of that!"

"That's what it sounded like to me."

"And you're overestimating the power of your dick."

"Nah, you're *underestimating.* I bet you told all your little friends about how a nigga that doesn't even have both of his feet gave you the best dick of your life.

Didn't you?"

Her eyes went wide, and she laughed yet again, and that visual, paired with the sound set off a foreign sensation in my chest. Even when it was over, her lips remained curved into a little smile, her eyes bright, and happy, and damn, I just couldn't help myself.

Reese melted against me when I dipped my head, pressing my mouth to hers. I slipped my hands underneath her hoodie, gripping her at the waist in an attempt to pull her closer. She let out a little moan as I eased my tongue along the seam of her lips, beckoning her to open for me, and she did. I took my time exploring her mouth with my tongue, savoring her sweetness. Pulling her lip between my teeth, sucking, biting, soothing, then back to her tongue to taste a little more. When I finally pulled away, she was breathless. Chest heaving, eyes darkened with desire, and I could damn near feel the heat coming from between her legs.

Her lips stayed parted as she looked up at me, her soft pants breaking the silence that punctuated the loud beeping sounds of the microwave going off.

I grinned, then lowered my mouth again, brushing my lips against hers before I drew back, and gave her ass another good squeeze.

"Let's eat."

We ended up lighting the fireplace.

Yeah, yeah, we were corny as hell, but whatever.

After we ate, Reese put on one of her dad's vinyls, and we settled on the floor in front of the fireplace with that bottle of wine she'd opened earlier.

"I can't stop thinking about that spaghetti," she sighed, taking a long sip from her oversized glass. I had my back up against her couch, and she was beside me, but turned in my direction, with her legs crossed.

I chuckled a little. "Get some more then, if you want it."

She shook her head. "I may want it, but I don't need it. I'll be mad at myself when I wake up bloated tomorrow. I'm just shocked at how good it was. That

Brielle must be some cook."

"Oh, give the six year old all the credit, huh?"

"Giving the credit where I'm *sure* it's due," she laughed. "Which brother is her father?"

"Mr. Bestseller."

She nodded. "Is that the one who was with you at the bookstore that day?"

"Yeah. Arranging a signing that he's going to do for an upcoming book."

"Oh wow!" She took another slow sip from her glass. "I've never read his stuff before, is it good? And tell the truth."

I laughed. "What? Yeah, his stuff is good. I wouldn't claim his ass if it wasn't."

"What does he write? Nonfiction? SciFi?"

I tipped my head to the side. "Uhh… hard to say, actually. He writes in a couple of different genres. Some literary fiction that deals with relationships, a couple of thrillers. One big reviewer called him a cross between Walter Mosley and Eric Jerome Dickey."

Her eyes went wide. "Wow. Those are some pretty big comparisons."

"Yeah. He hates that shit, but it comes with the territory I guess. Real talk though, he's good. I can bring you some."

She shook her head. "Nah, I'll purchase. Support his art. But I'm coming to *your* ass for my money back if I don't like it."

"Why me?!"

"Cause you made the recommendation. Is there any sex in his books?"

I laughed. "Yeah, in a couple."

"Write *those* titles down for me. That's what I wanna read."

"Are you serious, Reese?"

She giggled, then took another sip from her glass.

"Hell yes! It's getting cold out too? One of my most favorite things is curling up right here, with some wine, and a good book – if there's good sex in it, even better. So if your brother fucks up my vibe, you're gonna hear about it."

"Alright, alright. I can accept that. I'll get you a list."

"Thank you."

Neither of us said anything for a few moments, and Reese finished off her glass of wine. She grabbed the bottle, topped off my glass, and then poured the rest for herself. As she sipped from her fresh glass, her eyes raked over me, and then settled on my leg.

"May I?"

I didn't really know what she was asking, but I nodded anyway, finishing off my glass in one big gulp as she reached for the leg of my sweat pants. Her eyes stayed on my face as she tugged it upward, exposing my prosthetic.

"Is it weird that I think this is really cool?" she asked, cautiously running her fingers over the stylized metal.

I chuckled, watching the wonder on her face as she examined it up close. "Not really… mine is purposely designed to look badass. I had a few friends from my army days who did mechanical engineering once they left the military. They spun that knowledge into the biomedical field. I reached out to them, and let them basically experiment with me. Ended up with this prosthetic, that I actually haven't had that long, and a more functional one that I use when I go running."

"Running? So, you're pretty well acclimated to using it then?"

"Yeah. I've been using a prosthetic for about two years. I've only had this particular one for about six months though. But back to your question, trust me. I'd rather you think it looks cool than some of the *other* reactions I tend to get."

She lifted an eyebrow. "Which are…?"

"Freaking out. Feeling sorry for me. Treating me like I'm frail."

"Oh whatever, Jason. You look like the fucking Terminator, nobody is treating you like you're frail. I don't believe that."

I shrugged. "You'd be surprised then. The incident was a little under three years ago. I've been through surgery, physical therapy, learning how to use the prosthetic, all of that, and I've seen a lot of different reactions throughout that time."

"You did all of that here?"

"Nah. When they sent me back stateside, I was out in Cali. I actually loved it out there, and the engineering industry is booming. I came back home to be with my family while I do the school thing, but I might accept an internship, and go back when I'm done."

"Oh. Okay."

I'd been watching her fingers as the traveled over the lines and grooves of my prosthetic. But something about her inflection over those last words made me look up, and there was marked dejection in her eyes as she turned toward the fire, and swallowed the last bit of wine in her glass.

"Hey… what's up?" I asked, reaching for her hand, only to have her pull it away.

"Nothing."

I wrinkled my forehead, and that turned into a full-on frown when she suddenly got up and walked in the kitchen, grabbing the empty wine bottle and glasses as she went.

What the fuck just happened?

I followed her into the kitchen, grabbing her at the waist to turn her in my direction. "You gonna tell me what's going on with you right now?"

She gave me a crazy look, like she didn't know what I was talking about. "I'm good."

"But tell me what's on your mind anyway. You've *never* had a problem doing that."

"It's nothing, damn!" She pushed her way out of my grasp, then stalked over to the corner to toss the wine bottle in the recycle bin. "Just thinking too hard."

I chuckled a little. "No such thing."

Reese sucked her teeth, shaking her head as she turned to face me. "Um, yeah. There definitely is."

She set to work cleaning our wine glasses in silence, and then left them on the dishrack on the counter. I followed her into the living room, where she turned off the record player and carefully slid the vinyl back into the protective sleeve.

"Is this your way of telling me it's time for me to go?" I asked, sliding my hands into the pockets of my sweats.

Reese stopped what she was doing, her fingers frozen over the chrome handle of the glass cabinet. "So you *can* put two and two together, huh?" she snipped, then shook her head. "I'm not telling you anything, Jason. Do whatever common sense is telling you that you should do."

Well damn.

She closed the cabinet, and then stalked over to the fireplace and bent down, getting ready to turn the gas off.

"Hold up," I said, my stride unhurried as I walked over to her. I grabbed her by the hand, ignoring her slight resistance as I led her back to the couch.

"What are you doing?"

I smiled, then sat down, pulling her into my lap.

"You said to do whatever common sense is telling me to, so I'm going to sit here for a few minutes, and I want you to sit with me. Aiight?"

She didn't say anything, but she didn't move either, so I relaxed into my position on the couch. After several minutes passed, Reese loosened up too, resting her head on my shoulder. Still, neither of us said anything. I actually started getting sleepy again, watching the soothing crackle of the fire as I made lazy circles on her back with my hand.

"I feel really stupid," she said finally, mumbling the words into my neck. "I let my mind wander, today. While we were eating, and talking, and I started thinking… maybe this could be something. A not-just-aconvenient-booty-call something. And yes, I know how crazy that is, to already be thinking about that, but I got so excited, because it's been forever since I really *liked* somebody. Really, *really* liked somebody. So there I was, thinking too hard. Doing too much."

I frowned. "Okay, but those are just your thoughts. Make me understand the *problem.*"

"You're leaving. *That's* the problem."

I could tell she regretted those words as soon as they came out of her mouth. She actually sucked in a breath, and started to climb out of my lap, but I looped an arm around her waist, keeping her there.

"And now you see the other side of "saying what's on my mind". If I'm not insulting you, I'm spilling awkward, inappropriate feelings. Wonderful, right?"

"Goddamn, when you bring out "high-strung"

Reese, you really commit to it, huh?" Her eyes narrowed, and she opened her mouth, but I spoke again before she could. "Relax, girl. Shit," I chuckled. "To be so *observant*, you sure did miss that I said I *might* go back to

Cali. I've got reasons to stay here, too. My family is here. Auto manufacturing is growing in this area, so I could potentially build a career. And... there's the possibility of a lot happening in the course of a year that might give me more reasons to stay."

"I'm not asking you for anything, Jason. Just venting. Real, meaningful connections don't come easy for me, and it's scary to think about getting attached to somebody who might be moving thousands of miles away."

I pushed out a heavy sigh.

"See?" she asked. "This is why I said "nothing" when you asked me what was wrong. Now you probably think I'm some crazy stalker chick or something."

"No I don't. I think you think too hard." I repositioned her in my lap, so that she was straddling me, and tucked my arms around her waist. "Listen... I know what it's like to lose somebody that you care about. It stays with you, in different ways. Not to mention that shit with ole boy, and your friend. People you trusted. I lost my mother, I've lost friends. When you make connections, you don't want to let them go. I was in the military, princess. Your friends, mentors, lovers, whatever… you learn to live with the knowledge that they can be reassigned and sent halfway around the world, sent to war, whatever, at any time. You ain't gotta defend *those* feelings. Not to me."

If someone had tried to tell me a few months ago that I'd be tucking cynicism to the side to comfort a woman – *this* woman – I would have called them a liar. I wasn't this dude. I didn't do this type of shit. Except… apparently I was. And apparently, I did.

And it felt completely natural, in the most abnormal way.

For the first time since I left the military, here was someone that I could be myself with. I loved my brothers,

my father, they were family. The guys from Sammy's, the guys from the service center, they were all cool too. But somehow, I felt most at ease with a woman who had the unique power to completely infuriate me and turn me on at the same time. Somebody whose life experience was so far removed from mine that I was shocked to find out we even had anything in common. Reese would trade jabs with me without batting an eye, teased me about my prosthetic instead of defining me by it. She *got* me.

So… fuck it.

The *least* I could do was put her mind at ease right now.

"Just chill, okay? Let's see what happens."

She quickly nodded. “Yeah. I want to do that. I mean… we’re only halfway through fall semester, so you’ll be here until after spring at least.”

“Right.”

“And I could always sabotage you in mama’s class, keep you here to retake it in the summer.”

“Okay *now* you sound like a stalker.”

Reese laughed, and it brought a smile to my face to see the smile back on hers. She put her hands on either side of my jaw, and brought her lips to mine. The little kiss she gave was feather-light, and she did that over and over, grinning as her eyes swept over my face. They were still glossy with emotion, but she was over the little hump, moving back toward the playful, sexy mood she’d been in before.

I groaned as she flicked her tongue over my bottom lip, then grazed it with her teeth, a move that sent blood rushing straight to my groin. She opened her legs a little wider in her straddled position, so that she could move closer, pressing her heat right up against me as she slipped her tongue into my mouth.

She still tasted like wine, savory and sweet, as her tongue skated against mine in seductive, unhurried licks. A little whimper sounded in her throat as I slipped my hands underneath her hoodie, moving and caressing soft skin until they closed around her breasts. Her nipples had already pebbled into hard peaks, and she moaned again, a little louder, when I gently tweaked them between my forefingers and thumbs.

"I hope you're not starting something you don't plan to finish, princess."

She grinned at those words, and then moved away from my hands, dropping her face to my neck. She kissed, sucked, licked her way up to my jaw, and I was painfully hard by the time she made it to my ear. She teased me there with a soft flick of her tongue, and a kiss, before she murmured, "Oh, I definitely plan to finish."

That was all I needed to hear to snatch her hoodie over her head, leaving her naked from the waist up in the soft light of the fire. I closed my hand over one dark copper areola, and my mouth over the other, making her moan, and arch against me again. I outlined the hard peak with my tongue, then gave it a long, slow suck that made her press a hand to the back of my head, inviting more. I accepted that invitation and did it again, ending with a gentle tug with my teeth.

We played like that for a few minutes, giving the other breast equal attention before we stripped each other out of our clothes. When we settled back on the couch again, there was nothing between us except the thin material of a condom. We shared an "*mmmmm*" as she sank onto me, surrounding me in wetness and heat. My hands closed over her ass cheeks and squeezed, pulling her onto me deeper, and I dropped my head back against the couch as she purposely clenched her muscles around me.

Goddamn, she feels good.

She leaned forward, peppering my face with soft kisses as she began to ride me. I lifted my head, capturing her mouth to taste and devour as I looped an arm around her waist, keeping her anchored close to me. Her movements were measured, fluid as she rolled her hips against me, pushing her body up and down. Even when she sped up, she only lost her rhythm when I dipped my head, licking, kissing, sucking her hard nipples again.

Her hands gripped my shoulders, using me for leverage as she rode me harder, faster. I pushed my fingers between her legs, finding her clit, and used her wetness to massage it in tight, firm circles. She let out a loud, "*ahhh!*" and fell against my chest, burying her face in my neck as she continued to ride.

Her arms went around my neck, holding tight as I locked my arm around her waist, using deep thrusts to drive into her. "*Jaaay!*" she whimpered in my ear, then repeated again and again in helpless moans as she rocked against me, meeting my upward strokes with frantic movements of her own. I felt the quiver in her legs and tension in her hips just before she came. Reese melted against me, nails digging into my shoulders, her body gripping and squeezing to milk me out of my own release.

She didn't try to move, and neither did I. We stayed where we were, locked together, with her face still buried in my neck, and me still inside of her. After a while, our breathing slowed to a normal pace, and Reese finally lifted her head, looking up.

"Jay?" she said, and I met her eyes in surprise.

"Why'd you look at me like that?"

I chuckled. "Shocked you called me what I've *been* asking you to call me. You always call me Jason. I only get to be *Jay* when my dick is in you I guess."

"Only time you've earned a nickname, to be honest," she giggled, then laid her head against my chest again.

She shivered as I ran my hand up her back, then down again, letting it rest on her ass. "Hey, what were you about to say though?"

"When?"

"When you called me Jay."

"Oh!" She shifted against me again, wrapping her arms around me. "I was going to ask if you were ready to heat up that spaghetti again now. I'm hungry."

twelve.

"Reese. Reese."

"*Whaaaat?*"

Reluctantly, I dragged my eyes open, squinting against the growing light in the room. It couldn't have been later than seven or so, on a Saturday morning, and Jason was hovering over me, nudging my shoulder.

"I'm leaving, and I want you to get up and come lock your deadbolt," he said, chuckling as I batted his hand away.

"Just turn the lock on the knob."

"Nah." He nudged me a little harder, and then his hands were under the covers, pulling me into a seated position. "I need you to come and do the deadbolt."

I pushed out a heavy sigh, and let my head roll back. "Oh my God, come on. What do you think is going to happen?"

"I don't think anything is going to happen, because you're going to get up and lock this door behind me. I know you think your nice neighborhood is safe, but crazy folks are everywhere."

I pouted for a few more moments, but he'd already sufficiently ruined my sleep. I climbed out of the bed, still nude from the night before, and Jason groaned when I bent to snag a t-shirt from my drawer.

"Stop making it hard for me to get out of here this morning, princess."

I shot him a grin as I tugged the shirt over my head, leaving it hiked around my waist as I bent to get a pair of shorts. "Who said you had to?"

"Promise I made my brother," he sighed, his eyes glued to the bare juncture of my thighs as I shimmied into my shorts. "Told him I'd watch Bri again this morning.

He's on a deadline, trying to get his book finished. I'm already gonna be cutting it close on the time."

I poked out my bottom lip, then turned to pad out of the room. "Too bad. No pussy for you this morning." "You gave it all to me last night anyway," he shot back, following me out of the room. I grinned as he caught me around the waist, pressing a kiss to my cheek before he passed me on the way to the front door. When I made it there, he put his arm around my neck, pulling me in to kiss my forehead. "I'll see you later, aiight?" *What time?*

Where?

What day?

What should I wear?

"Okay."

He pressed a close-mouthed kiss to my lips, and then he was gone, and I drew the deadbolt behind him. I let out a little sigh once I was alone again. I still felt great, but Jason had a certain energy about him and now that it was gone, the house felt empty.

I shook my head.

Already in too damned deep, Reesie.

But it was his fault, for being all smart and fine and easy to talk to. How could I not feel drawn to that? The only thing I could do now was try not to drown in it.

I was heading into the kitchen to see what I could figure out for breakfast when my doorbell rang. I turned on my heels and walked back, unlocking and pulling open the door.

"Um, excuse the *hell* out of me – was that the fine ass army vet I just passed coming out of your driveway?" Devyn didn't wait to be invited in- she brushed past me, stepping into the foyer to take off her coat. "Well, answer me girl!"

"Yes," I laughed. "That was Jason."

"*Really?! Ayyyee!*" She slapped her hands together, doing a little hip roll in front of me. "I *knew* you loved me Reesie!"

She kept dancing, and I laughed as she grabbed my hands, making me join in. "What are you talking about Dev?"

"I asked you to get that dick again and you did.

Cause you love me."

I giggled as I pulled my hands from hers to lock the door, then grabbed her again to pull her into the kitchen with me. "I *do* love you, but that's not why I slept with him again, sorry."

"What better reason could you possibly have? I mean you swore you didn't like him, you two didn't get along—"

"I was wrong." I shrugged, then let out a sigh as I sank onto one of the bar stools.

Devyn raised an eyebrow. "Ya think? You were crushing on him before you knew him. Then you found out he looks like he does. And you found out that he can handle going full force, toe to toe with you. And the sex was amazing. And you've been talking about him for months. How could you *not* like him?"

"Exactly," I said, pushing my braids out of my face. "But the thing is, he's leaving when he finishes school. *Might be* leaving when he finishes school. And that's—"

"Tough." Devyn sat down at the counter beside me, and squeezed my hand. "You like him enough to see what happens?"

I nodded. "Yeah. That's what we agreed to do."

"Good," Devyn smiled. "I think that's a good decision. You wouldn't even be thinking about whether or not you'd still have a relationship a year from now if you didn't *know* his staying was in question. But really, any guy could pack up and move away for his job, family, whatever. So just think about it like any other budding relationship. Stop freaking out. We're still in our twenties. From everything you've told me, I think Jason is really good for you. A nice balance. Maybe the *best* guy you've chosen in years."

I lifted an eyebrow. "Maybe?"

"I'm holding back on making a definitive statement until I meet him for myself. And I expect that to happen sooner than later… right?"

"Right," I laughed. "What are you even doing here so early anyway? What time is your test?"

She let out a loud groan. "My test is at one, and

I'm here because you wanted to take your braids down, remember? I cannot study *any* more, so I'm here to help myself by helping you. Netflix and a braid takedown until

I have to go.'"

"Sounds good to me. But, I need to go take a shower, brush my teeth, all of that first."

Devyn wrinkled her nose at me. "Ew. Go ahead, wash your little pum-pum. I'll go grab us some breakfast and come back."

I perked up at the thought of breakfast. "Ooh, where are you going?"

She shrugged. "I don't know. What do you want?"

Hmmm.

"Oooh," I said, snapping my fingers. "You should definitely go to—"

- & -

JASON

"Batter Up," I said, putting a plate of food in front of my niece at my kitchen table. I'd taken her to the little food truck that served waffles with "interesting" fillings and toppings on one of my first days back in town. With all the traveling I'd been doing before I left the military, and then rehab and everything after, I hadn't exactly gotten to spend a lot of time with Brielle for her to know me very well. At first, she wasn't impressed, but the first trip to that food truck – something she'd never been to before – was all it took to get her to warm up to Uncle Jay.

But now she expected it every time I saw her.

And well… she was adorable, so obviously I made it happen.

"I couldn't get a plate, Uncle Jay?"

I shook my head at Justin as he dropped onto my couch, letting his head fall back against the cushions.

"Nope. You're not as cute as she is," I said.

I left Bri in the kitchen, dancing as she chomped down on bacon-covered waffle sticks and more syrup than she probably needed. The TV in there was on some colorful cartoon pony crap she'd begged to watch, so I went into the living room, and dropped into a seat across from Justin.

"What's up with you?" I asked. "I was expecting you to cut out of here as soon as you dropped her off. I thought you were on some tight deadline?"

"I am," he groaned. "Procrastinating as long as I can, because I hate this fucking book."

My eyes went wide, then shot over to Bri, who was blissfully unaware of the conversation. "What do you mean, you hate it?"

"I mean exactly what I said. I wouldn't even be writing it if I wasn't under contract for this last one. Still can't believe I signed a four book deal with these clowns."

"Wouldn't have happened if you'd stuck with Toni."

"Hey," Justin said, sitting up. "The hell did you just say?"

I scoffed. "I said it wouldn't have happened if you'd stuck with Toni."

Justin rolled his eyes, then dropped his head back down. "I don't want to hear that shit."

"Good thing I wasn't asking what you wanted to hear. Toni was good to you, and—"

"*Good to me* wasn't getting my books on bestseller lists, and Toni understood that. I did what I needed to do for my career."

"And look where you are now! Complaining because that big publishing house thinks they own you now, and your fancy ass agent got you locked into a crappy deal, and you have to finish this little wack series—"

"Wack? The series isn't wack."

I lifted an eyebrow. "The series is kinda wack. It's the *only* wack thing you've done, but..."

"But it's not wack."

"It's definitely wack."

Justin scowled. "It's *not*… shit." He groaned. "Yeah, the series is wack. Which is why I don't feel like writing this wack ass final book." He stared off into space for a few seconds, and then shook his head. "I should have listened to Toni."

"Yep," I nodded, as he stood up, looking dejected. "Definitely should have."

I stood up too, watching as Justin dropped by the kitchen to talk to Bri. He doted on that little girl, and as much as I rode him about the choices he'd made with his career, I knew he did it for her. He said goodbye to her, then planted a kiss on her forehead before he walked with me to the front door.

"Later, I want to hear about where you spent the night," he said, clapping me on the shoulder. "You *and* Pops."

My eyes went big. "Yo, are you serious? He spent the night at her house?!"

Justin shook his head. "Yeah, man. I don't know how to feel about that."

"Hell, *I'm* happy for him. Why wouldn't I be?"

"Because you haven't seen this woman, Jay!"

I narrowed my eyes. "And you have?"

Pops had been consistently tight-lipped about the woman in his life, and unlike my brothers, I wasn't bothered by that. They were concerned about somebody trying to take advantage of him, use him for money, but if I knew our father like I thought I did, I doubt we really had to worry about that.

Was he lonely? Yes.

Was he stupid? Hell no.

"You know I had you watching Bri while I had that dinner meeting with my agent, right? We're sitting at a table by the window, and who do I see walking down the street holding hands, necking like teenagers?!"

I tried not to grin. "Who, Jus?"

"Our father, and a woman half his age!"

Then, I did laugh. "How would you even know that? Did you ask?"

"I didn't have to! I couldn't really see her face, but if you'd seen the boots, the dress, and the body, you'd know what I mean. And early this morning when I drove by, his car still wasn't there."

I shook my head. "Come on, Justin. Stop tripping. So dad got him a little honey dip. Let him have his fun."

Justin let out a heavy sigh. "I don't know, man…"

"Good thing he isn't asking our opinion then, right?"

There was silence for a few seconds as Justin stared at me with narrowed eyes, and then shook his head. A moment later, he laughed. "You know what?

Yeah, you're right. I need to get some damn business," he chuckled.

"You really do. Would you even be in his business like this if you were writing a book you actually liked?"

He scoffed. "Hell no. I'd be in my characters' business instead."

I shrugged. "So there you go. Finish the book so you can move on to some folks you actually want to write about. Or you could get you a woman of your own..."

"Whatever Jay. I'll be back around three to get

Bri."

We exchanged a quick goodbye, and then Justin headed off. I went back inside to check on Brielle, and after breakfast, she and I kicked it hard. Cartoons on the TV, dolls and hexbugs on the floor, polish on the toenails of my prosthetic, which she was in awe of. After lunch, I left her mostly to herself with her tablet, while I set up my laptop on the couch beside her and finished the first draft of a paper for my Modern Black Lit class.

Which of course took my thoughts straight to Reese.

Not that they hadn't been already, but writing about this book – which I'd already read before and was one of my mother's favorites – brought her closer to the forefront of my mind. I wondered what she would be doing today. Was it too soon if I wanted to see her again later? Did I really care about "too soon" and other bullshit like that?

I forced my thoughts back to my paper, since the draft was due on Monday. A little after three, Justin arrived to grab Brielle, and I got dressed for my short evening shift at the dealership.

Lucky for me, I was in the service center today.

Most of the jobs were just tune-ups and normal maintenance, but even that was better than that salesman shit. I'd been back there for a couple of hours before Pops came by, looking for me.

"You got plans for dinner, son?" he asked, catching up to me as I climbed out of a car I'd just finished detailing.

I shook my head as I swung the door closed. I'd still been thinking about seeing what Reese was up to, but as of now, "Nah. Why, what's up?"

He pushed his hands into the pockets of his slacks. "Well, I wanted all you boys to come over tonight so we can eat and catch up. And… meet a friend of mine."

Immediately, a smile spread over my face. "A

"friend", huh? Would it happen to be the friend whose house you spent the night at last night?"

"How the hell do you know that?" His expression shifted into a scowl, and he crossed his arms over his chest.

I shrugged. "Streets be talking, Pops. Streets named Justin."

"That boy, I swear." Pops shook his head.

"He's just concerned about you," I said, clapping him on the shoulder. "Justin kinda took on most of the load when you were going through it right after Mom died, so he's protective. He did say she was fine though.

And that she was half your age."

Pops chuckled. "She's not half my age. She's only ten years younger."

"Still, she must be pretty damned bad if she's got you ready to introduce her to the family."

"Would you expect anything less from your old man?"

Shaking my head, I laughed. "Nah, I really wouldn't. So what time are we meeting your "friend"?" I asked, passing him to pick up the car's service history sheet from the metal counter at the front of the room.

"Seven-thirty."

I nodded. "Aiight. That'll give me time to go home and grab a quick shower."

"Good. She's got a daughter about your age, who she's bringing too. Pretty young woman…"

I lifted an eyebrow. "Me dating your "friend's" daughter would be kind of incestuous, wouldn't it? And besides, I already kind of have a… a… girlfriend." Before I could think of an appropriate term to use for what I wasn't completely sure was a relationship, Pops started laughing.

"What did I tell you boy? Hope you've got money for a ring."

I sucked my teeth. "Come on with that, man. There's not gonna be a ring any time soon."

"You sure?" He grinned. "Yesterday, you

"weren't even dating". Today, she's your girlfriend. Looks like things are moving pretty fast to me. I might mess around and get another grandbaby."

"*Chill*," I insisted, even though I was laughing.

"You playing, you might mess around and get your little young tender pregnant. Mess around and get me a sibling."

Pops shook his head. "Took care of that possibility long ago," he chuckled. "Last baby was twenty-eight years ago, and I sure intend to keep it that way."

"Yeah, yeah." I looked up at my father, and smiled at the joy on his face. "Seems like she's got you hooked."

He grinned. "Yeah, she does. Haven't felt like this since Cilla. Reminds me of when she and I first started dating. Your momma had me hooked too."

"That's all I need to hear then," I said, nodding.

"I'm happy for you. For real."

He bobbed his head. "I appreciate that." A few seconds passed without him saying anything, and I turned to my clipboard to start marking off the service items I'd filled for the car. "So," he started, and when I looked up, he had his head bent, kicking at a stain on the floor. "You don't think it's too soon? Feel like it's… an insult, to your mother? For me to date, move on?"

"Man, *hell* nah," I scowled. "None of us think that. We know how you felt about mama, know you loved her. It's been four years, Pops. I think even mama would want you to enjoy your life, and move on."

"Well I know *that*. She actually told me that, when she was sick. She knew it was coming, and she wanted me to promise not to waste away after she left. You boys are the only reason I could keep that promise though. I don't want you feeling like I'm disrespecting her memory."

"I don't," I insisted. "*We* don't. Don't even… Just erase that from your mind. You said seven-thirty, right?"

"Yep. Seven thirty."

"Aiight. I'll be there."

- & -

"Reesie get dressed."

My eyes popped open, and I screamed at the sight of my mother standing over the tub. I hadn't been expecting her, nor had I heard her come in, so her sudden intrusion into my relaxing bubble bath scared the hell out of me.

"Don't be dramatic," she said, before she turned to head out of the bathroom. "I didn't mean to scare you.

You weren't answering your phone or doorbell. I used my key to make sure you were still alive. And you had your music up too loud. I could hear it from my side."

I rolled my eyes as I pulled myself out of the tub. I'd already been in there nearly an hour anyway, and the water was starting to get less than warm. "What if I'd had company?" I asked, wrapping myself in a towel. When I stepped out of the bathroom, the light was on in my closet, and I found my mother there, flipping through hangers.

"Then I would have politely snuck back out and gone to my house to wash out my eyes. But I didn't see a car other than yours, so I assumed it was safe. I need you to get dressed, so we can go."

I lifted an eyebrow. "Go where?"

"To Joseph's, for dinner. With his family."

My mouth dropped open, and I quickly closed it back, letting my lips spread into a grin. "Ah, so that dress and those boots got you invited to meet the family, huh?"

She pulled out a sweater dress, looked it over, and then hung it up again before she turned to look at me.

"Just the boots," she said, then winked before she went back to looking through my clothes.

"Oooh, mama you're *nasty*," I giggled, gently nudging her aside to pick out my own clothes. "Is this dinner a formal thing, or…?"

"Casual," she answered, looking over my shoulder.

I grabbed a pair of jeans, then started looking for a top. "Okay. What time?"

"We're supposed to be there at seven thirty."

My eyes shot over to the clock. "Mama, it's 6:45!"

She shrugged. "I tried to call, and I sent a text message thing. Just throw something on, Reesie. It's dinner at his house. Look at me!"

My eyes raked over her, from head to toe and then back up, landing on her face with a deadpan expression.

My mother looked like she'd stepped out of a magazine, per usual, in boots, slim-fitting rust colored pants, and a thick, creamy off-white sweater.

I, on the other hand, was going to be ashy if I didn't put on some lotion *real* soon, and had taken down my braids earlier in the day. I'd only bothered with washing and conditioning my hair, and pulled it into a band on top of my head. Dealing with it would take at *least* an hour.

I groaned. "How long does it take to get to his house?"

"It's about fifteen minutes. Twenty to be safe."

I groaned again. "Okay, so… I've got twenty-five minutes. I guess I'll see what I can do."

I put the jeans back, and grabbed leggings instead, pairing them with a dark olive sweater and skirt combo. I lotioned and dressed quickly, then pulled on boots to keep it simple, and decided on big hoops and minimal makeup, since I really didn't have time. I lifted an eyebrow at my hair, pulled on top of my head, and frowned. No way I could tackle it if we didn't want to be late. I tugged open a drawer on my vanity, digging around until I found a narrow silk scarf, and tied it around my hair like an intricate headband.

I wonder if Jason is going to be there.

That thought hit me out of nowhere, reminding me that as far as *I* knew, he still didn't know my mother was dating his father.

When Jason and I were together, I honestly wasn't thinking about them. I was in the moment with him, focused on us… and was it really my place to say something anyway? I'd never discussed my mother's love life with previous boyfriends, but this was admittedly a little different since this time, she was dating my boyfriend's father.

Wait.

Did I just call him my boyfriend?

The word felt foreign, even in my thoughts. But as strange as it was, it also felt really, really… nice.

I thought about texting him, giving him some sort of heads up, and then decided against it. He hadn't texted or called all day, and I honestly wasn't sure what the right move was. Gray was the first, and only guy I'd dated since my father died, six years ago, and obviously, I hadn't handled that very well. Instead of stressing about it, I chose to finish getting myself ready so we wouldn't be late.

If nothing else, I'd see Jason there.

At 7:28, my mother and I headed up the front steps of a gorgeous two-story brick home. I was nervous like I was the one meeting my man's family.

Wait…

Technically… I *was*.

The door swung open, and there was Joseph on the other side, just as salt-and-pepper handsome as I remembered. He pulled my mother into a hug once we were inside, and she just melted, practically *purring* as he placed a soft kiss against her lips.

I watched them in awe, because they were obviously in love. And I wasn't the only one entertained – two tall-and-fines were standing at the other side of the living room, watching, amused. It didn't take much to deduce that these were Jason's brothers. Mama and Joseph separated themselves long enough to run through introductions.

All of the men shared similar deep brown complexions, with different features. Justin was the spitting image of his father, and Joseph favored, but had the same nose and brow shape as Jason, which must have come from their mother. I assumed Jason looked most like her, judging from the other men in his family.

A gorgeous little girl came bouncing across the room, with smooth deep brown skin and a head full of thick black curls pulled into two puffs on top of her head.

"I'm Brielle," she chimed, showing off deep dimples as she smiled. She was introduced to my mother, who she declared to look like a queen, which tickled mama.

Brielle turned to me, with her big brown eyes wide. "You're pretty!"

"Well thank you," I smiled. "And so are you! I like your dress."

"Thank you. You wanna see my hexbugs?"

I lifted an eyebrow. "Umm… sure? If it's okay with your father." I glanced up at Justin, who shrugged.

"Fine with me. Take it easy on her please Bri."

"*Okaaaay* daddy!" Brielle grabbed me by the hand and led me over to a kid-sized table set up in the corner. I kneeled beside her as she showed me a set of tiny robotic bugs, contained by a maze of tubes. I watched as she disassembled and then reassembled the maze with different paths, then started it up, giggling as the "hex bugs" ran through it, bumping and flipping and climbing over each other as they went.

"Did your uncle Jason get these for you?" I asked, and she turned to me with a big smile, and nodded. I smiled back. Of course he'd given her an engineering and robotics toy, nurturing her brain with science instead of just the typical dolls.

A few seconds after that, there was an influx of action as someone else came to the door. Jason's voice was soothing to my ears, as I heard him apologize to his father for running behind. I turned around just in time to see the shocked expression on his face as Joseph

"introduced" him to my mother.

"My professor, Pops? Really?" he asked, but seemed to be unbothered by it. They laughed through the introduction, and Jason expressed his surprise, but approval. And then he looked around, and his eyes fell on me and went wide. I pushed myself up from the floor, and stood.

"Hey Jason."

"Reese… hey."

Our eyes connected, and I could tell he was wondering if I knew before now. I gave him a subtle nod, and he frowned a little, then looked away. Suddenly, I felt almost… guilty.

Maybe I should have said something.

I didn't have time to think about it too hard before we were being ushered into the dining room, seated, and food was being passed around.

Of course I ended up seated next to Jason.

Everybody was talking, laughing, captivated as my mother explained how she and Joseph met. Jason's brothers asked questions, engaged my mother, and I was happy for her that they seemed to genuinely like her. And

I mean… why wouldn't they? It was obvious that she was completely enamored with their father. But Jason was quiet, which I hadn't expected.

Since nobody was paying attention to us anyway,

I reached under the table to grab his fingers. He didn't pull away, so I squeezed them, and he squeezed back, so I

looked up at met his eyes. "Is everything okay?" I mouthed, and even though he gave me a subtle nod, his eyes said something a little different.

Squeezing my hand one more time, he leaned toward me, and quietly muttered, "We'll talk." *Could he be any more ominous?*

From there, the dinner seemed to drag on forever, even though I was willing it to be over, and soon.

Internally, I was freaking out, trying to figure out what exactly I'd already done wrong. When everyone was done eating, the party moved back into the kitchen for dessert, and that was when Jason chose to pull me aside, into a small room off the wall.

"Are you mad at me?" I asked, as soon as we were alone, looking up to meet his eyes.

He shook his head. "Nah, not mad. I just… why wouldn't you tell me if you knew our parents were dating? I remember that day in the professor's office, when you found out that he was my father. Why didn't you just say something then?"

"I don't know. I mean, you and I were talking, connecting… I was more interested in that than discussing our parents. And I didn't think anything was going to come of me and you, so it didn't seem like a big deal. And then from there, it just wasn't on my mind. I didn't find out about dinner tonight until right before."

"And you couldn't shoot me a text?"

I shrugged. "I thought maybe it would be a cute surprise. And… you hadn't texted or called all day, so I wasn't sure where your head was anyway. If yesterday was just like… a fluke."

"What?" he scoffed. "Nah, nothing like that. I've just been busy. Babysitting, school work, *work* work.

And… a little bit of wondering how to approach things with you."

I smiled. "Oh, so big, strong, Sgt. Wright… gets a little nervous too?"

He chuckled, swiping a hand over his face before he pushed his hands into his pockets. "I guess. Maybe a little." He pulled a hand from his pocket, reaching out to tug at one of the coils in my kinky-curly puff ponytail. "I like this," he said. "I'm surprised, but I like it."

I wrinkled my nose at him. "Why are you surprised?"

"I would've thought you wouldn't let a nap anywhere near you," he teased. "And yet here you are with a head full of natural hair."

"I love my naps," I giggled, running a hand through my puff. "I can be bougie without a relaxer. I thought you of all people would appreciate it."

He lifted an eyebrow. "Why's that?"

"Your first paper. You complained that none of the women in Corey Jefferson's book had dark brown skin or natural hair, and that was when I knew I wanted you."

"It was more of an observation than a complaint. I love black women of all varieties. But back to you wanting me…"

I sucked my teeth. "Well, not *you*, but the author of the paper."

"So you liked it that much?"

"I did," I nodded. "That paper was the first thing that attracted me to you, sight unseen."

"Well shit, I need to write some more papers then," He mused, wrapping his arms around my waist. He pressed his lips to mine, soft at first, then deeper, slipping his tongue in my mouth as he pulled me closer to him.

"So you're not mad at me?" I asked, when we ended the kiss.

"Nah," he shook his head. "Not at all. I would have liked to know that my father and my professor were dating, but neither one of them said anything either, so it's not like I can be pissed at you. It's just… weird."

I shrugged. "It's really not. Only when you think about it too hard. And even then, it comes back around to *not* weird."

"And I know you're damn good at thinking about shit too hard, so I'll take your word for it," he laughed.

"As far as I'm concerned though, we're good. Just got some more learning and figuring out to do with each other."

I smiled, then pushed myself up onto my toes for another kiss.

"I'm looking forward to it."

thirteen.

"Shit!"

I stopped what I was doing to grin at myself in the mirror. I wasn't sure what Jason was cursing about from my bathroom, but it was still a good feeling to have him there.

It was a Thursday morning, and we actually both had class today, so we were navigating the small space of my room to get ready. We'd been dating for a month now, but this was the first intentional overnight stay during the week.

It was interesting.

In a good way.

Jason was very, *very* organized. I'd peeked into his bag, saw how neatly it was packed, and smiled. He packed better than *I* did.

"What's wrong?" I called, carefully tying a pretty scarf around the edges of my hair. I was fluffing out my fro when Jason peeked into the bedroom, still shirtless from his shower.

"Uhhh…"

I turned around. Something about the look on his face made a bubble of anxiety spike in my chest. “Jason, *what*?”

“That little dish on your bathroom counter…there was something in it, wasn’t there?”

“The purple one?”

He cringed. “Yeah.”

I swallowed hard, trying to get my heart out of my throat. “Yes. Yes, my chain that I always wear. Why?”

“Don’t freak out…”

I got up so fast I almost flipped over the bench at my vanity. “What do you mean don’t freak out?! What happened!?”

Jason sighed, swiping a hand over his face. “I… accidentally knocked it into the sink, and I thought I heard something in it, but the sink was empty, so I was hoping—”

“What?!”

I crossed the room while he was still talking, but I didn’t hear anything he said as I pushed him aside to get into the bathroom. Sure enough, the dish was empty, and my heart started to gallop as I looked over the counter, on the floor, in the trashcan, and didn’t see my chain.

Tightness seized my throat, and tears sprang to

my eyes as I turned back to Jason. “What the fuck happened?! The dish was on the other side of the counter, not even close to the sink!”

“Reese, chill. I put my towel down on the counter to put on my boxers. When I picked it back up, the dish and a couple of other things slid in there.”

"What kind of sense does it even make to put your towel on the counter, when there's a damned rack right behind the door? That wasn't just any necklace, Jason!

It's important to me!"

He scowled. "Why are you acting like I did the shit on purpose?!"

"Because it's lost either way!"

I scanned the bathroom one last time with bleary eyes, tuning out whatever the hell Jason was trying to say as I rummaged through the trash, dropped to my knees to check the corners, under the cabinet, everywhere. By the time I stood again, I was sobbing, and Jason was sitting on the edge of my bed, putting his prosthetic on.

"Reese," he called as I stormed past him, wiping my face with the back of my hand. I ignored him still, going to my vanity to look around there. I distinctly remembered taking it off in the bathroom to shower, and not immediately putting it back on because I was rushing to give Jason time. But still… maybe I'd picked it up and just didn't remember.

"*Reese.*"

Jason grabbed my arms, stopping my movements.

I struggled to get away from him because I didn't want to look at him right now, because that necklace was—"I can get it, princess. Calm down. Let me get my toolbox out of my trunk. Aiight?"

I let out a deep, shuddering breath as I tried to stop crying, but still didn't look at him. I sat down at the vanity as he grabbed his keys and left the room. A few moments later, he was back, and went right into the bathroom.

Ten years.

That's how long I'd had that necklace and never, *ever* lost it. My father had presented me with a delicate white box at my Sweet Sixteen, and I'd been in complete awe. My first real piece of jewelry, with a tiny plaque engraved with my name, and I felt *so* grown up. More than his record player, more than his vinyls, more than my *memories*… that necklace a real, touchable thing. Given in love, in warmth, attached to one of those beautiful memories. It was a tangible connection between my father and me, and the thought of losing it… I felt like my chest had been split in half. What if it was—

"Hey."

I sniffled as I looked up from my hands, and wiped my eyes. Jason was standing in front of me, still shirtless – had he gone outside like that? – holding out a dainty gold chain to me.

An unsteady breath flooded out of my lungs, and my shoulders sank in relief. I took it from him, covered in whatever gunk hung out at the bottom of the drain, and practically sprinted into the kitchen, my hands shaking as I washed it underneath the hottest water I could stand.

My fingers trembled as I grabbed both ends of tiny clasp, and lifted them around my neck. I tried and tried to make the two pieces connect, but my hands were quivering too bad.

"I've got you," I heard from behind me, and the ends of the necklace were gently pulled from my fingers. I dropped my hands to my sides, and a moment later, my little plaque was hanging in its rightful place at the base of my throat.

I closed my eyes, not bothering to stem the flow of tears that escaped my eyelids as Jason wrapped his arms around me from behind, pulling me to him as tightly as he could. "I'm sorry," he muttered against my ear, and I shook my head.

"It was an accident. I shouldn't have reacted like that, I just—"

"*Shhh.* You don't have to explain."

I turned in his arms, futilely attempting to dry my face. "But I do. It was a gift from my father, and… it means a lot to me. Maybe more than it should, but—" "*Shh,*" he repeated, using his thumbs to wipe my cheeks as I stared up into his eyes. "I get it. Trust me I do. My mother cried for days over losing an earring *her* mother gave her. I thought about that as soon as I saw your eyes well up."

"I didn't have to yell and curse at you."

He shrugged. "You didn't. And I started to make your mean ass wait, too." I poked out my bottom lip, and he chuckled, shaking his head. "Uh-uh, put that thing away. When I realized it was about your dad though, I knew I had to go ahead and get it for you."

"And I appreciate it. Thank you."

He wiped my face again, then pressed a soft kiss to my lips. "You're welcome. And I'm sorry for knocking it down in the first place. I probably could've been paying more attention to what I was doing.

"Ya think?"

Jason laughed, then swatted me on the butt. "So we're good?"

"Yeah," I nodded. "We're good."

"Good. You want to hit up Refill tonight?"

I lifted an eyebrow. "Are you asking me out on a date, Sgt. Wright?"

"I think I might be."

"On a Thursday night… don't you have classes tomorrow morning?"

He shrugged. "It's the only night Dani Renee is gonna be there, so…"

My eyes wide. "She's back!?"

"She's back," he grinned. "And since you missed her last time…"

Jason couldn't even get the rest of his words out before I launched into him for a hug. "Yess!" I exclaimed. "What time?!"

"Eight," he managed to say through my hair.

I had a big grin on my face as I pulled away, then entwined my fingers with his. "You are…"

"The most handsome, intelligent, funny, flat out *best* nigga you've ever dealt with?"

I rolled my eyes. "Well… you aiight, I guess."

"Ah, well. You probably don't want some little

"aiight" chump taking you out then, huh?" Jason grinned as I squeezed his fingers a little tighter.

"*Fiiine.* You're… a little more than aiight."

"Oh, I'ma show you *"aiight."*"

I squealed as he picked me up, tossing me over his shoulder to carry back into my room. We still had a little time before either of us had class, to have a little morning fun.

And then I'd call and find out if I was even *allowed* at Refill.

"So what exactly are your intentions with my friend?"

Oh God, here we go.

Jason looked taken aback by Devyn's question, and I couldn't blame him. She was sitting across for him at our booth style table, not cracking a smile as she stared at him, with an expression that was just barely neutral enough to not be a scowl.

"Um… I hadn't really thought about that much.

We're taking it easy right now."

She sucked her teeth. "Oh, so this is just casual to you? You're using my friend for your little freak-nasty needs, and when you tired, you're just gonna move on?" "I… *what*?"

"*Devyn*," I hissed, kicking her under the table.

"*Chill!*"

She kicked me right back. "Answer the question, Sgt. Wright. *If* you're even actually a Sergeant. What was your commanding officers name? In case I need to make some phone calls."

Jason turned to me, eyes wide. "Is she serious?"

"I'm asking the questions here," Devyn snipped, patting her hand on the table for attention. "Don't try to deflect."

Jason narrowed his eyes, and she narrowed hers too, lifting an eyebrow.

"Captain Derek Ingram was my commander at the time I accepted an honorary discharge. No, I don't intend to *use* your friend. And I don't think what we're doing is casual, it's just still relatively new. Ask me in six months what my intentions are, and I'll be able to give you a real answer."

Devyn's expression slowly softened. "Oh. So you plan to be around for the next six months, at least."

"Yeah, I do."

"Exclusive to her? Do you fuck your girlfriend's friends?"

Jason curled his lip. "What? *No.* I don't get down like that, and I don't make a habit of sleeping around."

"Mmmhmmm. Why do you like Reesie?"

I dropped my head onto the table, thinking about how thoroughly I was going to cuss her ass out later.

"She already knows the answer to that." I kicked Devyn under the table again.

"I wanna hear you say it."

Jason let out a heavy sigh, and even though my head was down, I could feel him sit back. "I like Reese because she's smart, funny, sexy, and not afraid to speak her mind. She's not afraid to be absolutely herself, and be open and honest. And I feel like I can be myself with her."

I lifted my head, just enough to turn to him.

"Really?" I asked, just above a whisper.

He lifted an eyebrow, giving me a look like I was insane. "Uh… yeah. Duh."

"Welll," Devyn said, her voice returning to the perky tone I was used to. "Congrats, Jay! As far as I'm concerned, you've passed the bestie-twin test… for now. Y'all cute or whateva'." When I lifted my head, Devyn was smiling, and she winked at me as she stood up. "I'm going to get a drink."

Jason turned to me as soon as she walked away

from our table at Refill, heading toward the bar. I'd called her to sweet talk big brother Eric into taking me off the banned list at the club – he never could say no to his baby sister – and she'd finagled her way into me agreeing to let her meet Jason.

Finally. – her word.

It wasn't that I was trying to keep them away from each other, or anything like that. I was trying, desperately, not to be a weirdo. Because of our unique circumstances, he'd already met my mother, which usually wouldn't happen until months into a relationship. I didn't want him thinking I was trying to integrate him into my whole family, especially after the way I'd had a mini freak-out over him possibly moving. The very last thing I needed was to sabotage this by making him think I was getting too attached.

I mean… there was a pretty good chance I was *definitely* already too attached, but he didn't need to know that.

"What the fuck was that?" he asked, leaning toward me.

I let out a loud sigh. "*That* was the bestie-twin test. She said you passed!"

"I thought you said she was "nice" bestie-twin?"

"She *is*," I laughed. "Just not during the test. Or when you piss her off. Or she doesn't like you."

He lifted an eyebrow. "So you two are just alike then?"

"No, no. She really is "nicer" than me. Devyn is generally bubbly, she's a little more talkative with people she doesn't know. She has a sweet spirit."

"Where?"

I gasped, then playfully slapped him on the arm through his sweater. "You'll see *that* side now that she's checked you out. She was harder on you because of Grayson."

"He passed?"

I almost choked on my drink as I lifted it to take a sip. "God no. She hated him from the moment she laid eyes on him."

Jason scowled. "So why do I get grilled harder because of him?"

"Because she's worried about me. Worried *for* me. But don't sweat it, seriously. She was a fan of yours before I was, and today just sealed that in."

"I'll take your word for it."

"You should," I grinned. "You'll see."

"Uh huh. You wanna get closer to the stage? I think Dani's about to go on."

"Hell yes, I do."

We headed up front with the growing crowd, Jason leading the way. With those broad shoulders, the crowd parted easily for him and then he pulled me in front of him, tucking his arms around me and resting his chin on my head.

I clapped and cheered with everybody else when Dani came on stage, looking beautiful with her cinnamon-colored locs and deep brown skin. She talked to the intimate crowd a little bit while her band did their last sound adjustments and stuff. And then the music started, and she began to sing, in that raspy-sexy, sensual voice of hers.

Ain't no easy ways to be in love, Sometimes you play the fool.

It's love and war, push and pull, And you try to play it cool.

When it's right, it's right, when it ain't, it's not

There's no one perfect rule.

You can play the game, and win or lose, Sometimes you get schooled.

Jason pulled me a little tighter against him, brushing my hair aside to kiss my neck. We stayed like that, swaying together to the music until Dani took a break, and we headed back to the table.

I groaned a little as I spotted Devyn's exboyfriend, Malcolm, seated at the table with her, speaking way too close into her ear. Malcolm wasn't necessarily a bad guy, but I wouldn't call him good either... at least not for Devyn.

I tried to fix my face into something that at least resembled a smile, but a few feet away from the table, my efforts got wiped away. I'd glanced up, and to my right, not looking for or at anything in particular, when my eyes fell on Grayson and Olivia.

Hmph. Trash sticking together.

I looked away almost as soon as my brain registered those words, hoping not to invite conversation—or confrontation. But that was obviously too much like right, because the next thing I knew, they were making their way over.

"So I see I was right about you and GI Joe," Grayson sneered, with Olivia peeking cautiously around his shoulder.

I couldn't even get my mouth open to respond before Jason's hand on my shoulder halted me, and he stepped between me and Grayson, folding his arms.

"Listen, man… I'm trying to have a good time with my girl. Everybody has moved on, let's just leave it that. No problem. And trust me… you don't want that to change."

Grayson's face wrinkled into a scowl. "Man, who are you supposed to b—"

He didn't get the chance to finish that sentence before Jason grabbed him by the collar, snatching him forward. It was such a subtle move that barely anybody in the semi dark club looked up.

"Nigga are you deaf?" Jason asked, his voice low, and edged in danger. "*This ain't a problem you want.*

Find something else to do." Jason shoved him backwards, out of our space, and then turned back to me as Grayson and Olivia… went and found something else to do, I assumed.

When we got back to the table, I wasn't even thinking about Devyn and Mal. I snuggled close to Jason in the corner of the booth, and he pressed a kiss to my forehead.

"Don't sweat that shit, aiight?" he asked, tipping his head to look me in the eyes. "Not letting them mess up our vibe."

I smiled, and shook my head. "Absolutely not."

And… we didn't.

Instead of thinking about old news, I focused on the current happiness in my life. Malcolm left the table, Devyn warmed right up to Jason, and before long, we were laughing, talking, and having a good time.

As it started approaching ten at night, we left. Jason and I had classes in the morning, and Devyn had an early shift at the county hospital – one of her last, since she'd gotten the job at University Hospital, and would be starting in a few weeks.

Jason and I held hands as we walked downtown, heading back to his car. He was telling me about this internship he'd applied for with a major car manufacturer, when the sickening crunch of metal on metal wedged in my ears, turning my insides to jello. I stopped walking and whipped around, my eyes bulging when I saw two cars smashed together, in the intersection Jason and I had just crossed. Nausea swept my stomach, and I clamped my mouth closed, trying to hold myself together.

"Reese? Reese, you aiight?" Jason's voice made me turn away from the jumble of metal, as other people began to gather in the intersection. In the distance, I heard sirens, moving closer. It wasn't until Jason squeezed my hand that I actually blinked. "You okay, princess?" *No.*

"Yeah," I said, forcing myself to smile even though my mouth felt like it was full of sawdust. He pulled me along, and I followed, though I felt like I was in a haze. In the car, he lifted his eyebrows in surprise when I told him I didn't want to go home, that I'd rather stay over with him. Still, he obliged.

We swung by my place first, so I could get my car, and get what I needed for an overnight stay. Back at his house, I showered and climbed straight into his bed. I snuggled deep under the covers with my fingers tracing the edges of the engraved nameplate on my necklace while I watched him put the finishing touches on a paper that was due in my mother's class tomorrow.

"Hey princess," he called, and I looked up, meeting his eyes. "Can you tell me if something sounds right to you?"

I nodded, then sat up a little further. "Yeah, sure."

"Aiight. So... *There's no point in this work where the reader is allowed to be comfortable – and that feels purposeful. Givens draws you out of your comfort zone with elegant prose, and then plunges you into grief right along with the unnamed main character as she navigates the impact of her sister's drug addiction on her own life.*

Tee, the sister, gets a name. By leaving herself unidentified, the narrator leaves us with a sense that she's distancing herself from the story, even though she clearly plays a part. But I don't believe this is the only reason she allows herself to remain unnamed. Through various points in the story, it is clear that the narrator isn't simply relaying the message.

She's in the room.

The night Tee sneaks out of the bungalow and runs into the Street Kings, the night the father sneaks into the bed, Tee's suicide attempt. The details are too vivid, the picture painted a little too clearly, for these to be secondhand accounts. There's a level of guilt hanging in every one of these words, begging the question of if the narrator's role in Tee's ruin is more than she lets on.

Maybe she leaves herself unnamed because she doesn't feel she deserves one in Tee's story." I was completely enthralled.

For those moments while he was reading out loud from his paper, I was wrapped up, remembering the very first of his words I'd read. This was no different – insightful commentary that was leaps and bounds better than a good three-quarters of the class. I knew because

I'd read most of their first drafts.

"That sounds really good," I said, sitting up. I was in one of his army tee shirts that I'd commandeered as my own after my shower, and I tucked it between my legs, concealing my nudity underneath. "Only a few people mentioned the narrator feeling guilty, which is actually a huge theme through this story, that not many seem to easily pick up on. So, I can tell you now that you'll definitely get points for that. Mama will be impressed."

He lifted an eyebrow. "She's not going to think you coached me on that, is she?"

"*Hell* no. My mother knows me well enough to know I'd be turned *right* off by needing to coach you through this.

You've been one of the strongest students from jump. She'll recognize your work when she sees it."

He nodded, then looked back at his laptop and let out a breath. "Yeah… I've got some stuff in here about the jealousy between the sisters, the abuse, the beating, all of that. How it led to Tee's addiction. A speculation that the narrator may have indulged in a little "white horse" herself, based on some of those erratic passages. I think I covered everything I need to."

"I think so too," I agreed. "Your draft was really good, and it sounds like you've made it even better, so… I don't think you have anything to worry about. But, you obviously are."

He grinned, swiping a hand over his head. "Yeah, I am. This paper is weighted heavier than all the others this semester, and after that low B on the first one, I need this shit to hit hard."

"And it will," I laughed. "Don't stress it. And don't tell *anybody* I told you this, but… at the end of the semester, she offers a chance to improve the grade on your lowest-scored assignment. You'll get a chance to pull it up – if you even need it."

"Yo, are you serious?"

I wrinkled my nose. "Yes. Why would I make something like that up?"

He shrugged. "I don't know, I have to ask with you. You know you like to sneak-attack. As a matter of fact… Are you going to tell me what's going on with you today? You haven't made any slick comments, no insults, nothing. What's up?"

My hands went up to my necklace. "Just… a weird feeling, after this morning. Thinking my necklace was gone really messed with my head."

And then that accident, I thought, but didn't say out loud. I didn't want to be dramatic, and still being shaken up about the necklace was bad enough. Jason closed his laptop and then came to the bed, leaning to give me a soft kiss against the lips.

"Well lets go to sleep them. Maybe tomorrow'll be better."

I nodded, then flopped back on the pillows as he left the room to get into the shower. I was half-asleep when he came back to bed, sliding under the covers with me and pulling me close. The warm comfort of his arms made it easy to drift off, into a deep sleep. But I was drawn from it suddenly, violently, by a loud, booming, rumble of thunder.

I sat up, realizing that my forehead was soaked in cold sweat. I extricated myself from Jason's hold around my waist, trying not to wake him. As soon as my feet hit the cold hardwood floor, unwelcome memories rushed to my mind. The screech of tires, screaming, the helpless limbo as the car spun out of control, and then, the sickening crunch of crushed metal and shattered glass.

I sucked in a breath, trying to bring the air back to my lungs, but it didn't feel like it was working. A flash of lightning, another monstrous peal of thunder brought back the merciless squeal of the wiper blades on the windshield, trying valiantly to keep the window clear. My father, cursing. Not because I'd called him to come and get me, because of the weather. Because of the storm that had cropped up out of nowhere.

I made my way out of Jason's bedroom on shaky legs, still struggling to breathe. It seemed like the harder I tried, the more my lungs constricted, the more nausea ripped through me. I looked around, frowning at my unfamiliar surroundings, and sank to my knees as my heart thumped erratically in my chest. Another roar of thunder, and I covered my ears, trying not to scream as heavy rain beat down on the house.

My eyes closed, but immediately wrenched them back open, shaking my head. I was back in that seat, back in that concrete drain, screaming for help, not for me, for him, and—

"Reese?!" I flinched as a hand came down on my shoulder, but didn't look up. Suddenly Jason's arms were around me, enveloping me in warmth. "You're having a panic attack. You're okay. Just breathe. Breathe, princess, breathe," he murmured in my ear, over and over, as his hands made soothing circles on my back.

I don't know how long he stayed with me like that, but eventually, I came back down. My breathing leveled, heart stopped racing, nausea dissipated. Little by little, I was able to calm down.

"Talk to me about what's going on with you," he insisted, but I shook my head.

"I'm exhausted, and we have class, and it's late. We can talk about it another time. Not tonight, please."

Jason let out a little sigh, but didn't push it. Once we were back in his bed, I snuggled close and cautiously closed my eyes, hoping to only see blackness. That hope was fulfilled – my desire for sleep was not. Jason managed to drift off, but I tossed and turned, shaken out of my calm by every clap of thunder or jolt of lightning. Instead of soothing, the sound of the rain was like nails on a chalkboard tonight, grating to my ears.

"Have you talked to anybody about this before?"

I flinched at the sound of Jason's drowsy voice in my ear. I hadn't realized he wasn't still asleep.

"Yeah," I said, nodding in the dark. "It hasn't happened in a really long time, but yeah… I talked to somebody. They gave me ways to cope, ways to get to sleep."

Jason grunted. "You *definitely* need some sleep.

You've been tossing for hours. Is there something I can do?"

"Not really. If I was home, I'd probably take some melatonin, and I have tea."

He sat up. "Give me your keys. I'll go—"

"Hell no!" I exclaimed, sitting up with him, blindly feeling for his arm. "You can't go out there in that."

"It's just rain, why—"

"Because it's not just rain! You can't go out in that storm, not for me. What if you… no. Just no, okay?

Please?"

Jason pulled away from me, and then suddenly the lamp was on, and his eyes were filled with concern as they scanned my face. "Reese… what aren't you telling me?"

"Nothing."

"Don't do that shit right now." He hadn't snapped at me, but his voice was firm as I looked away. "Just tell me."

I swallowed hard, closing my eyes as they welled up with tears. "I was in the car with him. I… was so stupid. Dating this guy who slipped something in my drink one night. But I knew as soon as I tasted it that something was off. I locked myself in a bathroom, called my dad to come and get me, and he did. I was the only one there once he got to house, boyfriend was gone. My dad was driving me home, back to my mom's when the storm started. Somebody hit us on the driver's side, so hard that the car rolled into one of those drainage ditch things."

Jason's face fell as he reached for me, pulling me against his chest. "I'm so sorry."

I sniffed, hard. "I know I'm not supposed to think this, but he'd still be here if it wasn't for me. I walked away without a scratch, and he—"

"Shut up," he rumbled softly in my ear. "I'm not gonna sit here and listen to you blame yourself for that. You did what you were supposed to do, call your father to get you out of a situation like that. It was *not* your fault that there was a car accident."

"I know. I *know*. But sometimes it really, really feels like it."

He drew me a little closer, holding me tight while I cried quiet tears. After a while, they subsided, and I buried my face against his chest.

"I'm not usually like this, I promise," I mumbled, my voice muffled against his skin. "The thing with the necklace, and then hearing that accident earlier, and the storm… It was just a tough day for me. I'm sorry."

He chuckled, then kissed my forehead. "You don't have to apologize for showing a little vulnerability, especially about something like this. Hell, I'm glad to see it. Reminds me that you aren't as Teflon-coated as you pretend to be."

"You trying to say I'm not tough?"

"That's not at all what I'm saying." I smiled as he used the pads of his thumbs to swipe tears from my face.

"You're the toughest princess I know."

"Why do you call me that?"

"What?"

"Princess."

Jason groaned, and then laid back. "I mean… that was my first impression of you. Sitting in front of the class, not saying anything to anybody except the professor, with this sophisticated look on your face.

Clothes, jewelry, shoes, always perfect. You already seemed to have that bougie vibe, and then we bumped into each other, and your reaction just sealed it in."

"My reaction?" I lifted an eyebrow, confused.

He rolled his eyes. "Yeah. You wrinkled that cute little nose when you saw my shirt, and immediately checked to make sure the dirty mechanic hadn't gotten anything on you."

"Oh my God!" I exclaimed, shaking my head. "It wasn't even like that! I mean, yes, I saw your shirt, and thought about motor oil, but it wasn't on some "ewww, dirty mechanic" thing. More like, "goddamnit, I knew I shouldn't have worn white, why the hell do I keep bumping into people today". Earlier that day, at lunch, I almost came to blows with this white boy dripping ketchup everywhere. I'll admit to some bougie, but I'm not *that* much of a snob. I was paranoid about my shirt."

Jason chuckled. "See? Princessy."

I sucked my teeth, and then reached over him to

turn off the light. "Whatever," I grumbled, and he grabbed me around the waist, pulling me on top of him.

"Hey… you okay?"

Even though he couldn't see me, I smiled, and pressed my lips to his. "Yeah. I'm okay." I let out a soft, inaudible sigh, thinking about how that might not have

been the case if I were at home by myself. Yeah, I'd dealt with the panic attacks before. Enough in the first few years after the accident to be somewhat used to them, even if it had been a while. I'd talked to therapists, who wrote down stuff like PTSD, and depression on their little pads. I'd gone through bottles and bottles of mood stabilizers, anxiety and depression meds before I got back to a reasonably good place.

I knew the anniversary of his death was a hard time, so I could prepare myself, know that I needed to stick close to the bed, use natural remedies to cope. Melatonin and tea, maybe some drinking, anything to avoid the stuff that made me feel like a zombie after.

Tonight had caught me way off guard.

"You think you're gonna be able to sleep?"

"Probably not. But I still don't want you to go out."

"Reese, you *need* to get some sle—"

I kissed him first, stopping his protest. "No," I murmured, gently nibbling at his bottom lip before I traced it with my tongue. I dipped my head, kissing his stubbled jaw, down to his neck. My hands drifted up over his chest, up to his ears, gently pulling and tugging.

He chuckled, trying to move his head away. "Don't try to distract me, woman."

"I don't know what you're talking about," I said, giggling as he flipped us over to rest on top of me. A contented sigh escaped my lips at the pleasant weight of his body on top of mine. I brought my hands up to his shoulders, resting them at the base of his neck as he lowered his lips to meet mine.

His kisses were gentle at first – soft, barely there. Little by little, the pressure increased, my lips parted, and our tongues met. Hands moved lower, gripping and squeezing and kneading my ass cheeks, pulling me against his growing erection.

I gasped a little as his hands moved under my shirt to cup my breasts. He tugged the soft fabric upward, exposing my breasts before he dove in, licking and sucking my nipples into hard peaks that he teased with his fingers as he kissed his way down.

Pressure was already building in my core by the time he eased my legs apart. He ran his tongue along the inside of my leg on one side, kissed the bare juncture of my thighs, and then licked his way down the other side. He peppered the insides of my thighs with kisses, nibbled the crease of my butt cheeks, building anticipation and making me wetter. I was squirming underneath his touch, anxious, ready to beg him to stop teasing when he pressed his whole tongue to me in a broad, slow lick, and then closed his mouth over me.

I nearly came right then.

My fingers raked over his scalp, and a highpitched moan escaped my throat as he lapped at me with his tongue. He perched my legs over his shoulders, burying his face between my thighs as he dipped his tongue in me, making slurping noises that sent a thrill of pleasure up my spine. Suddenly, he pushed my legs up higher, knees to chest, opening me up wider, noisily devouring me like I was the best thing he'd ever tasted. His mouth was everywhere on my slick flesh, sucking my lips, kissing, nibbling, licking me until my thighs began to tremble.

I tried to ease back, to calm my racing heart, quiet my yelps and moans of pleasure, but it was pointless with his arms locked around my thighs, holding me in place.

He licked me – savored me – until an orgasm wracked my body, leaving me trembling with joy.

Faintly, I heard him open the drawer beside the bed, and then he was between my legs again. His mouth came down to mine as he parted my thighs, sinking into me with a confident stroke that made me gasp. He plunged his tongue into my mouth as he began to stroke, giving me a sex-laced kiss that made me dizzy with passion. His tongue against mine, exploring, caressing, getting me high on him, if I wasn't already.

Something about being enveloped in nearly complete darkness made everything else more… intense. The sensually wet sound of flesh on flesh, his fingertips on my ass as he gripped and squeezed. His hot mouth on my neck, his breath in my ear as he growled about how good I felt around him.

For a while, his strokes were slow, measured, but eventually they picked up steam, until he was driving into me with deep, blissful strokes that made it hard to breathe. I hooked my legs around his waist, opening for him to get deeper, and digging my nails into his back when he did. His mouth went to my neck, sucking and biting as he burrowed himself deep, grinding into me. My eyes stung with tears of pleasure as I pressed my face to his shoulder, trying not to scream as he began driving into me again, with fast paced strokes that made me feel like I was right on the edge of combusting.

And then I did.

Jason's mouth crashed onto mine as I came, swallowing my scream of ecstasy. He slammed into me one last time a few moments later, groaning as he locked his arms around my waist, holding me tight against him.

Sleep came for me quickly after that. I felt Jason leave the bed to get rid of the condom, clean himself up, and then come back with a towel for me before he climbed back into the bed. I was barely conscious as he moved the warm terry cloth over my skin, more gentle than I would've been with myself, but I smiled. Who would have thought that our literally running into each three months ago would lead to *this*? Me, falling asleep against a man who so obviously cared for me.

I used the last bit of energy I had and turned to him, snuggling close against his chest.

"Hey," I murmured, with my eyes already closed. "Thought you only did that for people who "belonged" to you."

"What?" he grunted back.

Our conversation in my mother's office seemed so long ago, but it flashed in my mind. *"The other stuff is reserved for someone who belongs to me. You trying to belong to me?"* We liked each other, had had a *lot* of sex in the month since we started dating, but both agreed that oral sex was a whole other level of intimacy.

"You ate the cookies."

I smiled at the warm rumble in his chest as he laughed at that, and then moved a hand down to squeeze my ass. "I guess I did, huh?"

"Yep. All of them. Were you trying to send a message? I belong to you now?"

His hand fumbled a little in the dark, before he grabbed my chin, tipping it up so he could press his lips to mine.

"I think you already know the answer to that question."

fourteen.

JASON

"Come on. Get your lazy ass up."

"Fuck you."

"I'll let you do that later. But for *now*, get up.

Come on. The sooner you do, the sooner it'll be over."

Reese shot me a scowl, rolled her eyes, and then pulled herself up from her seat on the edge of the fountain. "Fine, lets go."

We ran for a few more minutes before she slowed down, but this time, she kept moving instead of completely stopping. The light jog would at least keep her heart rate up, and gave us a chance to talk.

"This is why you don't eat two sweet potato pies by yourself over Thanksgiving," I teased, jogging little circles around her, but being careful not to break her pace. "Cause then, you get mad at yourself, and ask your man to help you—"

"And you end up contemplating killing his ass for forgetting that *you* weren't in the fucking army like he was, and that this isn't basic training."

"Says who?" I grinned, ignoring a couple of the strange looks I got as we jogged across the Blakewood campus. I was used to people's reaction when I worked out by now, and hell – I'd probably be looking too if a big dude ran past me with one leg encased sweats and a running shoe, and the other replaced by my running prosthetic from the knee down.

It was early in the morning though, and still pretty quiet. Reese shot another scowl in my direction.

"Says *me*. You're pushing too hard, again."

"Nah, baby. You're tough. My baby thug, remember? You can snatch a chair from under somebody, you can take a little tough-love training. Now come on.

Move it."

I smacked her on the ass, hard, and ran past her, grinning at the murderous look she gave me. It accomplished my goal though, and she started running a little, and then a lot faster, trying to catch up to me.

A few minutes later, I stopped her, and checked her heartrate from the tracker on her wrist. "Aiight, let's walk a little bit. Let your heartrate come down before this last stretch."

Reese used the arm of her running jacket to wipe away the sweat that had built on her forehead. It was cold outside, in the late November weather, but we were more than warm enough from running.

"So… I heard back about that internship in Cali this morning," I said, carefully watching her face for a reaction.

She kept her eyes averted, head pointed to the sky as she sucked in air. "Yeah? What'd they say?"

"I got it. They were really impressed with my credentials… excited to have somebody who was former military. Asked me to finish spring semester at a school out there. Paid internship, with a job upon graduation.

And the salary is bananas."

Reese dropped her head, and tugged her lip between her teeth, before she looked up, turning to me with glossy eyes. "That's amazing, Jay. I'm so proud of you." She stopped walking to step in front of me, grabbing my face as she pushed herself up on her toes to kiss me. "That's really, really good. I'm happy for you."

I believed her. I could see the pride in her eyes, see the genuine delight she felt for me. Right behind the dejection she was trying to hide.

"Thank you," I said, grabbing her hand as she tried to pull away. "They were in my top three choices, so it's pretty cool that they actually made an offer."

She playfully rolled her eyes. "Oh please. You're *you*. They would have been crazy not to give it to you."

I tugged at her, trying to keep her still, trying to

get her to look right at me, but she wouldn't. Instead, she slipped her hand away from mine and turned around, quickly brushing her eyes before she spoke.

"Let's finish this up," she said, her voice carrying a slight strain that she cleared her throat to try to conceal.

"Let's race. Last mile."

I chuckled. "You really want to do that?"

"I can beat you."

"Yeah, sure. What do I get when I win?"

"I'll treat you to Batter Up."

I lifted an eyebrow. "Really, Reese? Waffles after a run?"

She shrugged. "If I win, you treat. Celebration breakfast for your internship." Yeah.

More like *comfort* breakfast, after the news I'd just dropped in her lap. Win or lose, I was paying anyway. "Fine. I'll count, because I don't trust you."

"Whatever Jason."

I shook my head as we walked to the next light post that lined the sidewalks of the campus. I looked at her for confirmation. "We'll go on three, aiight? You ready?" She nodded. "Okay. One. T—"

I *knew* she was going to do that shit.

My mouth was barely making the "T" sound before Reese shot off, at an honestly impressive pace. I blew out a deep breath and closed my eyes for a second

before I took off behind her. It didn't take me long to catch up.

I grabbed her around the waist, pulling her off of her feet. She screamed as I pulled her against me, planting a kiss against the back of her neck.

"Put me down!"

I obliged her demand, laughing at how hard she scowled at me once her feet were back on the ground.

"You know you forfeited by cheating, right? No Batter Up. Scrambled eggs and oatmeal."

She sucked her teeth. "Whatever. I'll probably be ending the night with a pint of ice cream anyway."

Reese pulled her hood up over the two fat cornrows she'd tamed her hair into. Not because she was cold, because she was trying to obscure her face. I talked to her, teased, tried to get her back to playful, but she was all one-word answers as we headed back to the car.

We were just a few feet away from the parking lot when I grabbed her hand again, pulling her against me. I tugged her hood down, bringing her face out, and I wasn't surprised that it was wet, or that her eyes were rimmed in red from crying. I brought my hands up, wiping her cheeks. "I don't think I'm taking the internship in Cali."

Her eyes narrowed in confusion. "What? How can you pass up that kind of opportunity?"

I shrugged. "It's a nice opportunity, but a company here offered something similar. Only difference is that the internship isn't paid, but that's not a deal breaker for me. I have savings, and it's only six months. I like it *here*. With my family, in the city where I grew up."

Fresh tears sprang from Reese's eyes as she shoved me away. "So you knew that, and you made me think you were leaving?!"

"I was just telling you about it! And… I won't lie. I wanted to see your reaction, see if you cared."

She twisted her face. "For what?! Is it funny to you?"

"No!" I scrubbed a hand over my head. "Not funny, not at all. I'm saying… I wanted to know how you'd be upset by the thought of me leaving, because you matter in the decision, Reese. If you'd been all blasé about it, that would've let me know that you're not wrapped up in me like I'm wrapped up in you. And that would have made it a helluva lot easier to leave!"

"So you *are* leaving!" Reese shook her head.

"Fifty times a day, I'm thinking about you, wondering about you, hoping that I'm showing you that I care! As much as I care about you, do you really think I'd be okay with you leaving? Is that the impression I've given, that I want to be without you? Cause I don't!" She covered her mouth with her hand, turning to walk away, but I caught her again.

"*No*." I pulled her flush against me, one arm around her waist, one hand gently gripping her chin.

"No," I repeated. I'd made that decision, just then. What sense would it make to move thousands of miles away, away from a woman who made me feel like Reese did?

We were barely approaching two months, but in that time, we'd grown so close that I barely remembered what it was like to be without her. We read, cooked, worked out, slept, chilled, damn near everything together.

She'd challenged and encouraged, nurtured and insulted her way right into my heart, and I was no expert on it, but… something told me she was the woman I was going to be spending my life with.

Not that I was going to be saying that shit out loud any time soon, but still. It mattered.

"I'm *not* leaving," I said one more time, just to reinforce it to her. "I'm taking the internship *here*, not just because I like it here, not just because I want to be around my family. Because I want to be around *you*, princess."

Her hard expression immediately softened, and she nodded, sniffling as once again, her eyes welled with tears. "Thank you."

I pressed my lips to hers for a kiss, and she eagerly kissed me back. Full tongue and everything, right in the middle of campus. We laughed our way back to the car, hand in hand, and as we approached the passenger side, Reese squeezed my fingers.

"Please don't ever scare me like that again," she murmured, looking up into my eyes.

I gave her a smile, then kissed her sweaty forehead. "I won't. I promise."

"Good. Cause I'm gonna kick your leg from under you if you do that shit again."

My eyes went wide, and met hers as she lifted an eyebrow at me. "What the *fuck*, Reese?" I laughed, shaking my head. "You are… I swear… I love you."

Her lips parted in a little gasp, and then the corners of her mouth tipped into a smile that made warmth blossom in my chest. "You have no idea how glad I am to hear that, Sgt. Wright. Because I love you too."

- the end –

If you enjoyed this book (or even if you didn't!) please consider leaving a review/rating on Amazon and/or Goodreads. Not only does it help others decide if they'd like to meet these characters, it's how I know you're out there, and I would love to know what you thought about the book!

You can also visit me at my website http://www.BeingMrsJones.com/ (you can email me there from the contact page), like my Facebook page, at https://www.Facebook.com/BeingMrsJones or connect with me on Twitter, at @BeingMrsJones.
Team CCJ – Love in Warm Hues – https://www.facebook.com/groups/160811935613 6737
Want updates on new releases and giveaways? Join my mailing list!

Christina C. Jones is a modern romance novelist who has penned more than 20 books. She has earned a reputation as a storyteller who seamlessly weaves the complexities of modern life into captivating tales of black romance.

Prior to her work as a full time writer,

Christina successfully ran Visual Luxe, a digital creative design studio. Coupling a burning passion to write and the drive to hone her craft, Christina

made the transition to writing full-time in 2014.

With more than 17,000 books sold or borrowed,

Christina has attracted a community of enthusiastic readers across the globe who continue to read and share her sweet, sexy, and sometimes scandalous stories.

Most recently, two of Christina's book series have been optioned for film and television projects and are currently in development.

Other titles by Christina Jones

Love and Other Things
Haunted (paranormal)
Mine Tonight (erotica) **Friends & Lovers:**
Finding Forever
Chasing Commitment
Strictly Professional:
Strictly Professional
Unfinished Business **Serendipitous Love:**
A Crazy Little Thing Called Love
Didn't Mean To Love You
Fall In Love Again
The Way Love Goes Love You Forever **Trouble:**
The Trouble With Love
The Trouble With Us The Right Kind Of Trouble
If You Can (Romantic Suspense):
Catch Me If You Can
Release Me If You Can Save Me If You Can **Inevitable Love:**
Inevitable Conclusions
Inevitable Seductions **The Wright Brothers:**
Getting Schooled – Jason & Reese
Pulling Doubles – Joseph & Devyn

Made in the USA
Lexington, KY
07 January 2017